A Place for Murder

A Novel By
DAVE VIZARD

Also by Dave Vizard

A Formula for Murder
A Grand Murder
Murder in the Wind

About this novel

This is a work of fiction. Names, characters, places, and incidents are either the product of the author's imagination or used fictitiously. Any resemblance to actual persons, living or dead, business establishments, events, or locales is entirely coincidental.

Credits

Edited by: Christina M. Frey, J.D., Christina@pagetwoediting.com
Cover photo by Bill Diller, bdiller924@hotmail.com
Back photo by Bill Diller, bdiller924@hotmail.com
Design and formatting: Duane Wurst, duane0w@gmail.com

ISBN: 9781790168149

Printed in the United State of America

Acknowledgements:

A Place for Murder is largely a Huron County production. This story could not have been created without the help of many hands. In addition to the very talented and skilled artists noted earlier in the book's credits, I relied on the experience, knowledge and expertise of many others throughout the area. My thanks to Janis Stein, Richard Bass, Dennis Collins, Michele LaPorte, Monica Facundo Garza, scott Meyersieck, and Teresa Calkins. My thanks to all.

Dedication

I will be forever thankful to the great teachers in my life who inspired me to become a journalist and writer. They encouraged me to reach high and aim for the moon. This work of fiction is dedicated to Mrs. Ewing, Mr. Warren, Mr. Coopes, Mr. Foote, Mr. Cudney, and Mr. Hamilton.

Chapter 1 — Wednesday afternoon

Nick Steele tossed the memo from the assignment editor up in the air and watched it flutter to the top of his desk. Desperate for a fresh idea, he had hoped the action might spark creativity. Nothing flashed to mind. He turned the memo over and put it on the mountainous pile in the corner.

The *Bay City Blade* news reporter decided to let the assignment settle for a bit while he grabbed a fresh cup of hot coffee, which was not likely to be fresh or hot, from the percolator located in the corner of the newsroom.

The contents of the memo rolled around and bounced back and forth across his mind as he walked. The memo said: "Nick, a farmer in Pinconning claims he grew a potato that looks exactly like former President George W. Bush." Nick's job: Go talk to the guy, get photos, and file a thousand-word story for tomorrow's paper. Deadline, five o'clock.

A thousand words on a Bush potato head? Nick thought. He needed a new angle. He wondered if the farmer had used a special fertilizer to get the Bush result. Manure, especially the kind from horses or cows, would be too fitting.

As he poured coffee into his mug, the smell of burned leather wafted from the coffee pot the closer he came to the bottom. He tossed the chunky liquid into the sink next to the percolator and looked for filters that would hopefully produce a better result from a new pot.

It was a Wednesday afternoon in the *Blade* newsroom. Wednesday is often referred to as the Dead Day because that's when the news cycle typically slows to a crawl. Many government agencies meet on

Mondays and Tuesdays, and most of the public mayhem takes place over the weekend or just before or after.

Copy editors and sports reporters had completed their early shifts and left for the day already. Now only a handful of reporters and a couple photographers milled around the cavernous office. Every so often, a ringing telephone broke the quiet of the newsroom. Nobody offered to help Nick with the coffee, but two grabbed their cups when they saw him priming the percolator.

As he made his way back to his desk, Nick recalled a similar assignment he received just before New Year's Day. A woman from the tiny hamlet of Crump called the newsroom and left a message that on Christmas Day she'd snapped off a photo of a cloud formation showing a smiling Virgin Mary cradling the baby Jesus, with Joseph and three wise men nodding approval in the background.

The problem? Nick could not spot Mary or the baby Jesus in the picture. Joseph and the wise men looked more like the jagged profile of the Rocky Mountains. Nick believed the woman was sincere, and he did not want to hurt her feelings by calling her a nutjob, psycho, or raving lunatic. He saved those adjectives for the people who truly deserved it—editors.

After careful thought, the reporter had handled the assignment by writing an article posing this question to readers: "What do *you* see in this photo taken by a local woman?" The Crump woman's view would be reported with a second publication of the photo—smaller, of course—in the next day's paper.

Reader response was overwhelming. More than three thousand people emailed or called the newspaper hotline to record their views. Only three declared that Mary and the baby Jesus dominated the image. The rest of the responses ranged from "It's Madonna with a guitar on her hip" to "I see a beautiful flower garden in the fluffy clouds."

The story and its follow-up the next day were such a big hit that *Blade* management created a regular feature called "What do you see?" Newsroom smartasses, who are never in short supply, called it the Wacko File.

At first the Bush potato head had been relegated to the Wacko bin, but the daily news cycle had run dry of interesting stories. *Blade* editors, desperate for copy, had pulled Bush out of the file and assigned it to Nick, who was part of a newsroom rotation to handle such stories.

The percolator had almost finished its job when a reporter called out from across the newsroom to Nick, "Hey, Steele, call on line one. Want to take it, or get a message?"

Nick asked who was on the phone.

"Guy says his name is Nate, and he's calling from Mackinac Island," the reporter said. "Do you want him to hold?"

Nick scooted across the newsroom, eager to chat with Nate again and hoping to avoid the potato head caper.

"Hi, Nate," he said, catching his breath after the sprint to his desk. The burst of activity reminded him how out of shape he had become. "How the hell are you? What's happening on the island?"

Nick had met Nate while looking into a murder at the Grand Hotel two years earlier. Nate trained and handled horses at one of the biggest liveries on Mackinac Island. He'd found Nick partially clothed in his horse barn and reeling from an epic hangover after a disastrous game of beer euchre with a group of local old farts at the Mustang Lounge. The two had become fast friends and stayed in touch.

"I'm good, Nick, thanks. You okay these days, or are you still hittin' the sauce and running around in your underwear at night like a crazy man?"

Nick laughed and said he was doing fine. "What can I do for you?"

"I've got some bad news," Nate said, pausing to let that sink in for a moment. "Remember Suzie Alvarez, the sweet gal who worked at the Grand and got into a passel of trouble?"

"Yes, I do, Nate," Nick said. Suzie had been suspended from her job as a maid for breaking hotel rules. She had unwittingly helped a murderer slip past security, an unforgivable blunder. "Is she still working on the island summers?"

"No, and it's bad. Really bad. I'm saddened to say they found Suzie's body in the back of a pickup truck between Traverse City and Mackinaw City," Nate said.

Nick's mood darkened at the news. He sat up in his chair and flipped the telephone receiver to his other ear, urging Nate to continue.

"Nick, it just broke my heart. They cut her throat and cracked open her skull. She was such a sweetheart. Can you help?"

"Oh my God, Nate. I'm so sorry," Nick said. "You bet. I'll be on the island in the morning. You can fill me in."

"Oh, and there's one more thing."

Nick steadied himself and shifted the phone back.

"The medical examiner said it was obvious she had been buried before they found her in the truck."

Chapter 2 — Thursday morning

Fortunately Nick's editors supported a run to northern Michigan to find out what happened to Suzie Alvarez, the young woman who had caused a stir on Mackinac Island two years before. The reporter thought it would make an interesting news story, and he wanted to help Nate.

Nick arrived in Mackinaw City midmorning, hopped an Arnold Transit Line Ferry to Mackinac Island, and spotted Nate waiting for him on the docks after the thirty-minute ride.

It was hard to miss the horse handler in the crowd waiting for the ferry. He was the consummate cowboy working on an island playground for the affluent. Nate stood long and lanky, dressed in cowboy boots, jeans, a leather vest, and a big, floppy, sweat-stained Stetson. He pushed the Stetson back on his head and leaned on a rail fence. A quick flick of his tongue shoved a toothpick to a corner of his mouth as the reporter neared.

Nate had worked on Mackinac Island for more than twenty years and had become a father figure of sorts to many of the young migrant workers who worked summers on the island, including Suzie Alvarez. Their mutual love of horses meant Nate took Suzie's demise particularly hard.

The two shook hands. "Hey, Nick, glad to see you, but I sure wish it was under better circumstances."

Nick nodded in agreement, offering the cowboy a firm grip and warm smile. The two men walked the short distance to the tourist district downtown in search of coffee and a bench. They found both at a corner street vendor's outpost.

The September morning sun warmed their bones, and the light

breeze off Lake Huron kept the buzzing blackflies aloft. Hundreds of tourists filled the downtown sidewalks, moving like cattle, keeping to the right, and marching together in each direction. Most dressed in shorts and T-shirts and soft walking shoes. Sunglasses and ball caps completed the look. They chattered among themselves and window-shopped, sometimes breaking off from the slow-moving herd to actually go into a store.

Nick loved people watching, but Nate would rather have been back at the stable, Nick knew. Horses were more predictable and loyal than people, he often said, and the natural beauties were a whole lot better to look at. With no motorized vehicles, except for emergency rigs, allowed on the island, horses were pivotal to most aspects of Mackinac Island life.

Nick sipped his brew and asked Nate to update him on Suzie Alvarez. She'd been suspended from work at the Grand Hotel after loaning an employee uniform to a woman who said she wanted to surprise her boyfriend with a fantasy visit to his hotel room.

Suzie agreed to help and accepted a hundred-dollar tip—also a violation of hotel policy. The situation turned ugly when the stranger donned the uniform and persuaded the room occupant to let her in, then drugged him and tossed him off the balcony like a bag of dirty laundry.

At first the death was thought to be accidental or a possible suicide. Nick's reporting revealed that the occupant of the room had been misidentified: the assassin had killed the wrong target. Pandemonium broke loose at the hotel and on the island. With Suzie's help, investigators were able to get a description and an artist's sketch of the killer.

After that, Suzie took a low profile and avoided questions about the incident. For a while she bounced between the large resorts on Mackinac Island, trying to pick up as much work as she could. Suzie

cleaned rooms, bussed tables, hosted cocktail hours, did laundry—
any work she could find. But the part-time wages barely covered
living expenses.

Seasonal workers on Mackinac Island make up a small army.
Year-round residents number some five hundred people, who could
not possibly meet the needs of more than a million visitors each
year. Suzie was one of about three thousand guest workers brought
onto Mackinac Island each summer. They come from all over the
world under the H-2B visa program, which controls the number of
immigrants who enter the United States to work temporarily.

But when Suzie was suspended and lost her primary sponsor,
she was supposed to go back to Mexico.

"Problem was, she had nothing to go back home to," Nate said,
slurping hot java from the lip of his cardboard cup. He stopped to
admire a passing team of horses pulling a wagon and pointed to the
pair of chestnut mares as they clopped by. "I trained them two—
they got the best dispositions on the whole island."

Nick leaned forward to get a look at Nate's pride. "Yup, they're
beauties, all right. But what do you mean about her not having anything to go back to?"

The cowboy returned his attention to Nick. "No family, no job,
no place even to put her head down," Nate said, wriggling on the
hard seat for another comfortable spot. "I felt real bad for her—we
all did. She made a big mistake, like a lot of kids, but it cost her. She
was desperate. We learned about her death from a three-paragraph
article in the *Record-Eagle*. Three paragraphs—they give more space
than that to wedding announcements."

Nick could see how much it bothered Nate that Suzie's death had
been deemed largely unremarkable. It also bothered the cowboy that
no one from law enforcement had visited Mackinac Island to gather
information about Suzie, find out why she had not gone home after

losing her job, or ask how she had finally gotten off the island.

Nate explained that Suzie's parents, who were farmers, had passed in a house fire several years ago. Her brother, Cesar, was older and had come to this country and joined the US Marines sometime before that. He was killed in an ambush before their parents died—a devastating blow to the whole family, though they knew he gave his life fighting for something and a country he believed in.

Suzie's only other sibling worked as an assistant manager in a world-class hotel in Acapulco. The sisters had dreams of building a life together in the resort business, possibly in the United States.

"Got some more bad news for you," Nate said.

"What's that?"

"Suzie's sister is here to ship her body back home," Nate said. "And she is really hot."

Nick's jaw fell open. He was surprised that she was in Michigan. "Hot as in attractive?"

"Hot as in madder than hell," Nate said. "She is a spitfire and as unpredictable as a mustang. Once you get to know her, you'll like her. She's eager to meet you."

"Wonderful. I can hardly wait." Nick swallowed the last of the cooled coffee and tossed his cup in a trash bin. "When does that happen? I need to brace myself for the storm."

Nate said Nick could meet Suzie's sister, Monica Alvarez, in Traverse City as soon as he could get there. "She says she's going to find out what happened to her sister, even if it means she's got to walk across a bed of hot coals barefoot. She is one determined woman."

The two were interrupted by a boisterous but proud troop of Boy Scouts who marched past them on their way to their annual service camp at Fort Mackinac. The youngsters sang and banged drums as they marched.

As the banging and yelping subsided, Nick asked Nate if he knew where Suzie had gone when she left Mackinac Island.

"I did some nosing around and found out she connected with a woman who offered her farm work and paid off her bills," Nate said. He handed Nick a slip of paper with the name of a boat and its captain, telling the reporter that as island rumor had it, Suzie had hitched a ride off the island on *Empty Pockets* with Captain Ned. "You can usually find him down at the docks. That's all I know."

Nick thanked Nate and said he would check the docks before he headed for Traverse City. He asked if the cowboy had any more advice. He was also curious why Nate had called him instead of the authorities.

"Oh, we've shared all this with the law," Nate said, brushing dirt from the side of his jeans. He leaned forward, elbows on his knees. "But most of us don't believe the people in power will put much effort into it. Suzie's just another dead Mexican to them—a body that nobody claimed until her sister showed up. Who would care? That's why I called you. Figured you'd give a damn and know how to get to the bottom of it."

Nick said he understood, though he could not guarantee how long or how far he would be allowed to chase the story. He did, however, find it intriguing. Suzie's death was anything but routine. Her killing was vicious and brutal, and he was curious why a body would be buried in the wilds of northern Michigan and then dug back up before being abandoned. And was there a connection, he wondered aloud, between Mackinac Island resorts and the farm operations that paid off resort workers' debt as a lure for employment?

"See there," Nate said, a toothy smile erupting across his craggy face. "You're already asking the right questions. Knew this would get your dander up. But there's one more thing. The law had trouble identifying her at first. No ID on her body. No fingerprints and no dental records."

Nick leaned back in his seat without speaking. He searched Nate's face for more information. "Well, then, how did the authorities identify her?"

"Her breasts," Nate said. "They identified her by her breast implants."

Chapter 3 — Thursday afternoon

As the Mackinac Island public docks came into view, Nick reached into the breast pocket of his jacket for the slip of paper the cowboy had given him. Scrawled on the thin sheet was "*Empty Pockets*, Captain Ned." No last name, no description of the boat.

The reporter looked out over the harbor, which was dotted with more than 150 vessels, some moored to the docks and many others anchored offshore. The harbor master's shack was empty. Captain Ned could have been any one of the hundreds of sailors working on the boats strung out in the beautiful bay—or he might have been out fishing.

But none of that deterred Nick. It was a great place to be out walking and get lost in the moment.

At first he'd wondered if the Mackinac Island assassin had tracked down Suzie and eliminated the only person who could identify her. But he thought that unlikely because it was such a messy killing. The assassin's method of operation was to research her victims and make their killings look like accidents or natural deaths.

Another thing that bothered Nick was the plastic surgery. It didn't make sense to him that Suzie would have breast implants, which were relatively expensive as far as he knew. She was young and poor and trying to pay for an education back in Mexico. Even if she had the money, why would she spend it on cosmetics?

A salty-looking old bird, complete with a Harley Davidson headscarf, mirror shades, and four days of gray growth on his face, approached. He wore a sleeveless T-shirt with the name of an obscure rock band on the front and blue jean shorts that had so many holes, they looked like they were held together with string.

This was a guy who belonged here, Nick thought, raising his right hand to chest level to slow Headscarf for a few questions. "I'm looking for Captain Ned," he said, smiling and moving slightly into the stranger's path.

"Don't think I know him." Headscarf stopped to lean against a dock post. Nearby gulls took flight, their wings flapping against the wind. He wiped a thin layer of saliva from his lips with the back of his hand. "Is he permanent or transient?"

"Not sure. He pilots *Empty Pockets*—ever heard of it?"

"Hmm, maybe." Headscarf scratched his whiskered chin with thick, stubby fingers. "Might be one of the fishing rigs. Go all the way down the docks and hang to your port side. Ask around. Somebody will point him out to ya."

Nick nodded his appreciation and walked toward the end of the docks, wondering whether port side meant left or right—a natural question for a stone-cold landlubber. As he passed moored boats, he casually checked their names, hoping to strike gold. Lots of colorful and interesting names but no *Empty Pockets*.

In front of Nick, a boy of about twelve cast a fishing line out past an open boat slip, scattering a half-dozen cormorants diving in search of lunch. Nearby a tall, slender woman was coiling a water line in front of a pleasure boat. Nick thought she looked strong as she whirled the hose in a circular motion, her hips swaying in rhythm with the hose. Nick's lingering attention prompted her to look up.

"Hi. Wondered if you could help me locate a guy named Ned," Nick said. "He captains *Empty Pockets*—just talked to a guy who thinks it may be one of the fishing boats."

"Who wants to know?" She finished her task with the water line. "You're not from around here. What do you want Ned for?"

Nick responded by identifying himself. "Just looking for some basic information. I'm not trying to cause trouble. Do you know how I can find him?"

The woman studied Nick, looking him up and down with her hands on her hips. She had short, spiky hair and wore a tattered red sweatshirt with khaki shorts that appeared way too tight to be comfortable. The reporter could tell she was trying to figure out how much information to reveal.

"Well, he's out on a job," she said. "He had to make a run up past St. Ignace and the island. Should be back later this afternoon."

"What kind of a job? Not much beyond St. Ignace and the island," Nick said. "Is he running his charter today?"

"That's something you should ask Ned—none of my business what he's doing up that way."

Nick thanked her and said he'd be around most of the day. "Where does he dock? Is he transient?" he asked, borrowing from the question Headscarf had posed to him moments earlier.

Khaki Shorts pointed to the end of the docks with her chin. "He usually takes a slip down there. Ned works out of Grindstone City in the Thumb, but he takes private charters and jobs all over Lake Huron. This is a good spot for his business."

As Nick walked away, he could hear Khaki Shorts telling someone that a nosy reporter was looking for Ned.

"Not good," a man's voice replied. Nick was dying to turn around and see who was speaking, but he slowed down instead, hoping to hear more. "Ned don't like strangers, and he's sure not going to be happy about talking to no reporter."

After more than twenty-five years as a newsman, Nick was used to the idea of people not wanting to talk with him. But he thought it a little odd that a guy who ran a charter boat wouldn't be interested in getting some free publicity via a news article. The *Bay City Blade* had a daily circulation of about fifty thousand subscribers and many more readers in northern Michigan.

As he neared the shore, Nick could hear someone running on the dock behind him. It was Khaki Shorts.

"Hey, *Empty Pockets* just cleared the break wall at the entrance of the harbor," she said, slowing to catch her breath. "Ned will be pulling up in a few minutes. Better catch him while you can. He may be heading back out."

Nick spotted the vessel moving toward the docks, slowing as it coasted into its slip. They watched the guy on the boat throw a line to another on the dock.

"I don't blame Ned for not liking strangers," Nick said, keeping his eyes on *Empty Pockets* as he and the woman walked over to it. He noted the name on the bow just above the boat's identification number. "I don't trust 'em either."

Khaki Shorts smiled and waved at the man getting off the boat. "Ned, this guy here is looking for you. I figured he was okay."

Ned and Nick shook hands, though the captain didn't look comfortable. He was short and heavy, built like a defensive lineman. He had a full dark-brown beard too, which Nick thought looked hot for the end of summer. The reporter tried to put him at ease as quickly as he could.

"Hey, Ned, don't want to take too much of your time," Nick said, identifying himself as a news reporter. "I wanted to ask you about someone you gave a ride to a while back."

Ned grunted and looked past Nick to survey the docks. "I give a lot of people rides, lots of them one way." The captain hitched up his dark-brown work pants by their belt loops. His navy-blue T-shirt declared in bold white letters that he'd rather be fishing.

"You might remember this one," Nick said. "Young Hispanic woman, about twenty years old. She would have been traveling alone. I never met her, but I hear she was quite striking—medium height, medium build. Suzie Alvarez."

Ned's face brightened as if a memory had popped to mind. He smiled. "Yeah, sure, I remember Suzie. Real nice kid. Said she was broke, needed to find work."

Nick relaxed a bit. He'd broken the ice with Ned. Hopefully the captain would ease up and talk freely, he thought. The two men sat down together on a bench, and he asked Ned where he'd taken Suzie.

"I dropped her at the public docks in Port Austin," the captain said. "Last I saw of her, she was walking down the dock toward town."

Nick asked Ned if he wanted to get a cup of coffee, offering to buy in the hope that hot java would extend their conversation. The captain declined with a shake of his head, saying he'd already drunk his fill for the day. The two watched Khaki Shorts as she walked back to her boat. She held their attention, no commentary necessary.

"You said Suzie was broke," Nick said at last. "Do you remember how she paid you?"

Ned removed his ball cap, revealing a drastically receding hairline and pale white skin that must not have seen the sun in ages. He scratched the side of his head with dirty fingernails that Nick thought looked chewed.

"She didn't. Her fare was paid before she got on my boat."

The remark caught Nick by surprise. He turned to face Ned. "Who covered her fare?"

"A woman named Janene," Ned said. "She has me do transports for her every so often. Pays cash up front, doesn't like a bunch of questions—but that's okay with me. I don't like a lot of questions either."

Nick took the hint. "Just one more and then I will leave you alone. You've been very helpful, and I appreciate it. Can you describe Janene?"

"Nope, never met her," he said, craning his neck to see what Khaki Shorts was doing down by her boat.

"What about a last name? Do you have Janene's last name?"

"You said one more question, then you hit me with another," Ned said, starting to stand up. Nick took that to mean their conversation was quickly coming to an end. "Never seen her, and I don't know her last name. I just get an envelope at the harbor master's shack with instructions and cash. Easy. I like that."

Nick asked if he could get a cell number from Ned in case he needed to talk with him again. Ned brushed off the request, saying he moved around a lot and would be hard to catch up to. "Just leave a message with the harbor master in Grindstone or Mackinac. I'll try to get back to you."

Not a lot of information to go on, but at least Nick had a partial name. Now he had to track down a woman named Janene, who was somewhere in the Thumb. It seemed unusual to Nick that a boat captain would work for someone he knew little about—or perhaps Ned, fearful of strangers, knew a lot more than he was revealing.

Chapter 4 — Late Thursday afternoon

Monica Alvarez struggled to keep her composure at the funeral home in downtown Traverse City as the chief mortician detailed the pile of paperwork that would have to be completed before she could ship her sister's body home.

Getting Suzie back to Mexico was not going to be as simple as placing a quick call to FedEx for special delivery. No way. Sending a dead body across the country and into Mexico was going to cause a sizable headache and a lot of cussing before the deed was done. Legally transporting or disposing of a body were not easy tasks. Lots of paperwork and red tape—a job that not many wanted to handle.

The funeral director's voice turned into monotonous murmuring. He droned on: Monica needed a certified copy of the death certificate, a Michigan burial transit permit, a Secretary of State statement containing the Great Seal of Michigan, and a notarized statement from the funeral director verifying that embalming had been completed. All documents had to be finished in Spanish, in duplicate, and presented to the Mexican consulate in Detroit. Then, once the documents were completed and approved, Suzie could be placed in a sealed casket or a hermetically sealed shipping container for transport.

Whew! Monica, head bowed, dabbed at her eyes with a soggy tissue. The funeral director pulled two more sheets from the big box on his desk and handed them to the young woman without speaking to her.

"What's this all going to cost?" she asked. "Give me the economy package."

"Air transit from Traverse City to Mexico City would run you about ten thousand dollars," he said, his voice dropping from the medium-pitched drone to a slow, somber baritone. "Of course, financing and a payment plan could be worked out."

"Are you crazy?" Monica said, the flood of tears suddenly subsiding. "Ten grand just to get her home? Forget that. I've got a better idea."

The woman, short and thin with long dark hair and eyes the color of a couple of eight balls, pulled out her cellphone to call a cousin. She spoke rapidly in Spanish before clicking off the phone.

"Hector is getting in his van right now," she said, her voice sharp. "He and his brother will drive straight through to pick up Suzie. Hopefully I can get this paperwork done before they arrive."

"I understand completely," the director said, moving in closer to her and dropping his voice to an empathetic whisper. He tried to cup her hands in his, but she recoiled at the move. "It can be very expensive. We'll have her ready to transport on our end. But I must caution you that every state has its own laws and guidelines on transporting bodies. I would not want to see you break the law."

Monica stared at the undertaker without commenting. The weight of taking care of her sister's remains was hitting home, and to top it off, Monica was in a new country, meeting with strangers. Luckily her English was first-rate, a source of pride for her. As an assistant manager at a major international resort in Acapulco, she worked hard at learning English. She was also fluent in French and German.

Monica explored the wadded tissue her fingers passed from hand to hand and back again. When she finally spoke, her emotions poured out. "Well, what choice do I have, really? We've got to risk it. Hector will have to drive with caution, and we will have to pray for a safe journey home. Ten grand is out of the question. We will figure out how to make it work."

The office door creaked open, and the receptionist leaned into the room and nodded to Monica. She announced that a gentleman named Nick Steele had asked to speak with her.

"I don't need a gentleman. I need a nasty son of a bitch," Monica said, passion rising in her voice. "I want someone who is willing to get down and dirty to find out who killed Suzie."

"Then I'm your man," Nick said, poking his head into the office. "One mean son of a bitch reporting for duty."

Monica smiled. The funeral director's mouth fell open. The receptionist gasped. Silence filled the room as Nick stepped forward to shake Monica's hand. Suzie's sister glanced over her shoulder and told the funeral director she'd be in touch. Then she and Nick walked out the door.

Monica felt an instant connection to the reporter, who was old enough to be her dad. A burly beefalo with broad shoulders and silver hair and a two-day growth of whiskers, he looked like a big panda bear, Monica thought. She felt at ease with him, which was a good thing. But what she wanted from him was much more than that. Above all, she wanted results.

So far, Monica had not been impressed with the law enforcement she had met. In her view, the Emmet County sheriff and the local prosecutor had already made up their minds about Suzie—some kind of drug deal gone bad. They seemed too casual about her sister's case. No one was pushing hard to get answers, and every official she had met, except for the regional medical examiner, was swamped with work. Monica wanted action and answers. She wanted justice for Suzie and peace of mind that her sister's killer, or killers, would not get away with murder.

Nate had given her hope that this reporter from a midsized paper could help her with the biggest challenge of her life. But she was curious if Nick would truly commit to solving her sister's case or whether he was simply interested in reporting a salacious story. She prayed for substance, not superficiality.

The two sat at a picnic table in a nearby park overlooking Grand Traverse Bay, which offered one of Michigan's most tranquil views. Sailboats danced in the breeze across the bay. Crystal-blue water, bright, warm sunshine, and the hilly contours that shaped the horseshoe inlet leading to Lake Michigan made a peaceful setting for some serious talk.

Monica saw no reason to waste time. She got right to the point and challenged the reporter. She asked why she should trust Nick when others had given her family such little attention. "What makes you different?"

The woman's directness caught Nick off guard. He leaned back to measure her, unsure if she was sincere or playing a game of discovery with him. Not too many of the people he interviewed turned the tables on him and questioned his motivations and integrity. He offered a flippant response, which he quickly discovered was a mistake. "What makes me different? Well, I put my pants on—and take them off—two legs at a time, and I'm a world-class beer drinker."

Monica's eyes flashed like a crossing signal at a railroad track. "Wrong answer. I don't need a smartass or a drunk as a partner," she said. "I think we're done here. Go play with someone else's life. Not mine."

She stood from the picnic table so fast that Nick thought he might be in physical danger if she got her hands on something blunt or sharp. He put up his hands, a signal to cool down, not one of his surrender. "Whoa, whoa. Hold on there a minute," he said. "What makes me different is that I care about the people I work with, and I invest my energy and skills in them completely. In addition I am, without doubt, among the best news reporters in the business."

Certainly, Nick had the professional awards and accolades to back up his claim. But he had never been a journalist who lived for praise from his colleagues. His joy came from helping people who were getting steamrolled while trying to live decent lives.

For a moment he wondered if Monica was too wounded from the shock and horror of the brutal loss of her sister, whose mutilated body was still stretched out on a mortician's table just blocks away. Perhaps she needed time before she could move forward.

She took a deep breath, and Nick thought her shoulders sagged. Monica studied him with laser eye contact. But after a few moments she sat back down at the picnic table across from the reporter and cleared her throat.

"Nate said you were a good journalist and that I could trust you," she said, leaning forward and linking her fingers on the table. In the span of a few seconds, she had gone from woman on fire to woman at peace. "Nate has been terrific. He tried to help Suzie on the island. I like him."

Monica stood and moved to Nick's side of the picnic table. She sat down, facing him. They were inches apart. "He said you were a bulldog and not afraid to step on toes to get answers."

"Nice of Nate, but I'm really just old, and I've been doing this so long that I simply do not give a damn about what people think," Nick said, smiling broadly. "He told me you were a spitfire. I think we'll get along fine."

Nick asked her to bring him up to date, starting with when she had last heard from her sister.

"About six months ago," Monica said. She described a frantic call from Suzie, who believed she was in danger because of information she had discovered about unlawful activity involving migrant workers. Suzie had no one to report the information to and did not know where to turn.

At the time, Suzie had been working on a dairy farm in the

Thumb of Michigan but was being moved across the state to work in fruit production. As soon as the orchard owner paid off her tab, she told Monica, she would be allowed to leave the farm, where she worked long hours, had few privileges, and made very little money. Suzie seemed excited for the change and promised to call when she got established in a new location.

Nick pressed for details—where Suzie had been and whom she'd had contact with. Did Monica know the farms where Suzie worked, or even the names of nearby towns? Where did she grocery shop? Did she attend church services? Where did she receive medical care? Did she have friends?

Monica pulled a notebook out of her purse and flipped through its pages. "Suzie mentioned a nun who would bring communion and look after the farm workers. Sister Sharon," she said, turning to a new notation. "She also had made friends with another female farm worker, someone even younger than she was. Maria, I believe. No last names."

Monica knew little beyond that. Their conversation was brief, she said, and she could hear others in the background waiting to use the phone.

The reporter asked who had contacted her when they found Suzie in the back of the truck. She nodded toward the funeral home. "He said he had bad news about Suzie," she said, turning back to the scenic view of the bay. A young windsurfer wrestled with his sail while trying to turn and ended up going for a swim. "No one had claimed her body, and they were ready to bury her without services."

Monica stood again and walked away from the picnic table toward the water. Nick could see her shoulders quaking and heard her weeping. He did not know her well enough to offer comfort with a hug, but he asked if she wanted to resume their talk later.

"No, we have no time to waste," she said, the tears drying as quickly as they'd started. She rejoined Nick, who had moved from the shaded area into the sunshine. "The medical examiner saw she had breast implants and removed them. A serial number took them to a plastic surgeon in Muskegon. Suzie had filled in my name and number as next of kin on the paperwork for her operation."

Monica searched her purse again, producing a small white handkerchief. She turned away from the reporter and blew her nose loudly twice, pausing to breathe deeply between honks. Nick did his best not to notice, but nearby geese scattered to the furthest point of the park at the sound of her relief.

"Were you aware that your sister had had the implant procedure?" Nick asked.

Monica shook her head and gave the reporter a look of disdain. "I cannot imagine her doing that," she said, becoming animated, gesturing with her hands. "No way in hell. We're not boob people. Look at me. Do I look like that's important to me? That's not what we're about. It's just extra fat on your chest. We would never pay for anything like that."

"Well, somebody did," Nick said. "They don't do 'em for free. Who paid for it?"

"The medical examiner didn't ask that question."

Nick needed more details than Monica could provide about how and where Suzie's body was discovered. He also wanted to talk to the Emmet County Sheriff's Office and the medical examiner. He asked her to contact both county offices and give them authorization to talk with him.

They both jotted information into their notebooks and tucked them away. Nick said he would be leaving Traverse City right away. He wondered if she had a picture of Suzie she could share. Monica returned to her purse and pulled out a color photograph of her and

Suzie celebrating Monica's latest promotion at the Acapulco resort. The dark-haired beauties sat side by side, an arm wrapped around each other's shoulder.

"Well, you're definitely sisters," Nick said, studying the photograph. "You could be twins."

"Everybody used to say that," Monica said, and she was smiling now. "We did everything together from the time we were kids growing up on the farm. Inseparable."

Nick did not say anything. He watched her savor the moment in silence. Then she blinked away tears and pressed the photograph into his hand.

"Find the bastards who took Suzie," she said. "The police aren't going to waste any time searching for the killer of a migrant. They couldn't care less. It's up to me. I'm going to see this through, but I need your help."

Nick nodded. "Let's search for the truth, then, and get some answers."

Chapter 5 — Friday morning

When Nick walked through the back door of the *Blade* newsroom, reporters were already banging away on their keyboards as time ticked off the deadline clock, which hung conspicuously and ominously above the office of managing editor Drayton Clapper. The reporter scanned the room, searching for the beefy chief, known as the C-Man.

Dave Balz, a reporter and Nick's longtime friend, caught up to his partner before he had a chance to sit at his desk. Dave had a bevy of questions for Nick. He was eager to learn what had happened to Suzie Alvarez, he said, and he wanted to know if he could help with the story.

"Hey, I ended up with your Bush potato head story," Dave added, plopping his large, round behind on the corner of Nick's desk. "It's turned out to be pretty funny. Seems the guy also has a squash that looks like Bill Clinton and a melon that looks like Hillary. I swear! I'm not kidding. We've got photos."

Nick was tickled to see Dave getting a kick out of the story. He promised to update Dave on the Alvarez story as soon as Clapper reappeared in the newsroom. Dave said he was trying to avoid the C-Man because he was on another tangent.

As Nick pawed through the pile of notes and memos on his desk, a voice boomed above the din of the newsroom, "Steele, Balz, my office. Now!" The C-Man marched through the newsroom, the rolls around his waist shimmying as his thick, stubby legs churned along. As usual, the chief's entrance into the newsroom caused a stir. Reporters and editors alike made sure they looked engrossed in their work—whether they were or not.

Clapper cuffed his shirtsleeves while hovering over his desk.

His striped tie hung loosely around his neck. He put his hands on his hips, revealing damp sweat rings shadowing his armpits. From the C-Man's demeanor, Nick knew somebody was in trouble. He hoped it wasn't him.

"Balz, I'll start with you," Clapper growled. "What the hell is wrong with you? All the years you've been in this business, and you moon the mayor on Washington Avenue in downtown Bay City in the middle of the day? Are you a complete moron? Have you lost your damn mind?"

"She deserved it," Dave said, defiant while mounting his defense. "Mayor Newsham cast the deciding vote against the marijuana referendum. A good mooning was called for, and she knows it."

"Horseshit. You're suspended," Clapper said, so angry that spittle seeped out of the corners of his lips. "You can come back after you apologize to the mayor, though I doubt telling her you're sorry will wipe the image of your hairy ass from her memory bank. She could be scarred for life."

"You can't suspend me. I'm retired," Dave said. "I'm only here to give this place some class. Plus, you love having me in the newsroom."

"Get out of here before I call security."

"Please do," Dave said, and slowly walked to the front of the newsroom for what Nick knew was dramatic effect. Then he announced loudly, "The last time you called security, I went out drinking with the guard all day. If you call him today, we'll probably go to the mayor's house and smoke dope in her driveway all afternoon."

Clapper ignored Balz and motioned for Nick to follow him to the conference room. He asked Nick to hold off on the Suzie Alvarez update until the daily news meeting so they could fill in the whole team at once. The two walked to the big conference room, which had filled with department heads and copy editors.

The daily news budget meeting brought all factions of the newsroom together to plan coverage of major events and present the best news offering from each department for the next day's paper. Articles, photos, and graphics from the sports, lifestyle, national, international, business, and local news departments were discussed openly. The C-Man would then make the call on the display. Meetings typically lasted an hour but sometimes went longer if debate flared.

The hallmark of any good newsroom is diverse opinion and wide-open discussion. Journalists must hear all sides of an issue and discuss it openly without fear of reprisal. But healthy debate sometimes drives the discussion to areas that are uncomfortable even for the most open-minded.

When Clapper entered with Nick trailing behind, the conference room went silent in anticipation. It had been a slow news week, and all were eager to hear details on the gruesome death of Suzie Alvarez.

Just as the door was about to close, Dave scooted in and took a seat in a corner out of the C-Man's view. Being in the chief's doghouse was not going to put him off the story. Nick happened to catch Dave's entrance out of the corner of his eye and gave him a discreet wink.

"Before we get started with our regular meeting, I thought it would save us a lot of time to have Nick give a quick update on what he learned from his trip Up North," Clapper said. "We can discuss, then cut Nick loose before we continue our meeting. Nick, the floor is yours."

The reporter rose from his chair and scanned the room. All eyes were on him. He recounted in general terms what he had learned from talking with Nate and Monica. He also revealed the basic information contained in a news release from the Emmet County Sheriff's Office.

According to the sheriff, a body identified as Suzie Alvarez had been discovered in the back of an abandoned pickup truck off U.S. Route 31 near Paradise Lake, just south of Mackinaw City. The body had been covered with a tarp. The victim had a severe head wound and her throat had been cut. Drugs were not discovered at the scene, but needle marks were found on the victim. The body was being released to family members and would be transported back to Mexico. No arrests had been made, but deputies were continuing to investigate.

"Now, we all know that's how every cop news release ends— 'police are continuing to investigate'—and they usually do," Nick said. "But my initial inquiries into the Alvarez story indicate that this case is not among their highest priorities. In fact, I'm hearing it's already been shelved and labeled drug and/or gang related."

Nick said he was eager to go back Up North to dig further. What he had learned so far told him there was much more to this story than the gruesome death of one young woman. "Too many things about this case don't add up," he said. "Something else is going on here. I need some time to see how the pieces of this puzzle fit—or don't."

A long silence fell over the men and women assembled in the conference room. Nick thought he was finished with this discussion, but he was wrong.

After a moment, the sports editor raised his hand. Attention shifted to Richard Head. Clapper acknowledged him. "What's on your mind, Rich?"

"Okay." Rich cleared his throat and stood up to make his point. "Tell me again why we care? Why are we devoting resources and time to look into the death of an illegal alien? She is not part of our community. She doesn't belong here. She is a lawbreaker, and she would have been deported if she had been captured before she was killed. Why are we even pursuing this story?"

The sports editor's comments sent a low rumble rolling across the conference room. Clearly, Head had hit a nerve. Reporters and editors whispered, not so quietly, among themselves. The chief did not react immediately, but he had a ready answer for those who agreed with the sports editor.

"We've already written about her," the C-Man said in an even, matter-of-fact tone. He slowly scanned the entire room before continuing. "She was part of the story Nick did about the Mackinac Island death. What was his name? Zimmerman? So, I think a follow-up story is a natural. People who read about his death in our paper would be curious to know what happened to one of the key players in the story."

Nick nodded in agreement. He added that Suzie had met what looked like a violent death while living in the newspaper's circulation area. That alone, he said, merited pursuing the story to discover what happened to her, regardless of her citizenship. "We would certainly write about someone from Norway who met a violent death while in our community."

The sports editor was not moved. "Well, it's pretty obvious why she's dead. It's gotta be drugs," he said. "Those people are always dealing drugs. Looks to me like she got what was coming to her."

"Wait a minute, wait a minute," Nick said, his voice rising. He stepped away from the C-Man at the conference room table and moved toward the sports editor. "What do you mean by 'those people'? Are you suggesting all Mexicans are drug dealers? That's a stereotype, and it's racist."

Another murmur rose across the conference room, and Nick was surprised to hear a fair number of newspeople agreeing with

Richard. Still, others disagreed sharply.

The *Blade*'s sole Hispanic employee, a photographer who was born in nearby Saginaw, stood to make a point. "I don't like where this discussion is headed," he said. "Just because the victim is Latina does not mean she was running drugs or would be part of drug culture. As far as I know, drugs don't discriminate in who they enslave. I know plenty of people of all colors and from all cultures who are its victims. What I'm hearing in this room is a little scary."

The C-Man thanked Paul for his input. He noted that the *Blade*, like so many other news-gathering operations across the country, did not employ many minorities, which was unfortunate. Still, he wanted to hear all points of view from those assembled.

It quickly became obvious that the *Blade* staff was not going to be bashful about sharing their opinions. A page designer spoke in support of Paul, urging others to keep open minds and focus on the crimes committed—not on fulfilling stereotypes. That prompted more debate, even from staff members who were usually quiet as mice in the newsroom.

"I would be willing to bet that if you checked our clip files, you would find that every throat slitting in our circulation area over the last ten years was related to drugs," said a female copy editor, who wore wire-rimmed glasses and avoided making eye contact while speaking. "I think Rich is right. Why should we do anything for illegals? I say deport them all and solve our drug and prostitution problem."

"Wait a minute, who said anything about prostitution?" Nick asked, agitated by the kind of questions and insinuations bandied about the newsroom. It made him more determined than ever to dig into the story. No matter what, he thought, the truth had to come out.

"Rumor around the newsroom is that she was identified by her breast implants," the copy editor said. "Why would she have fake boobs if she wasn't a hooker? That's all they are good for—hooking men and emptying their wallets."

Men and women in the room were now openly arguing with each other. The lifestyle editor rose from his chair and said he was worried about a trend. "What if this is the beginning of a wave of illegal immigrants spreading across the state like locusts, devouring everything in its path?" He suggested the *Blade* write a tough editorial against illegal immigration and this potential infestation. He also thought a series of articles about immigrants, regardless of status, might be in order.

Those remarks drew condemnation from another copy editor, who decried them as dehumanizing to people who were only seeking what everyone in the room already enjoyed: economic opportunity and freedom from oppression.

The murmur rose to a deafening din. The Suzie Alvarez story had struck a nerve. The freewheeling discussion from all factions of the newsroom also was an indication to the chief that the subject matter would very likely prompt a similar fervor across the community.

"Okay." The C-Man rose and lifted his hands to chest level, palms down. The gesture called for calm and did its job remarkably well. "Good discussion that will definitely be continued," he said. "Thanks, Nick. You can go put your story together for Saturday's paper. Then let's talk before you head back Up North."

The reporter nodded, picked up his notebook, and headed for the door. Dave slipped out of the conference room right behind him, barely able to contain himself as the two headed down the hallway back toward the newsroom.

After what he'd heard in the conference room, Nick thought he needed Dave's help on this story more than ever. He believed his partner would add a level of reporting know-how, tenacity, experience, and raw instinct to chase down a thorough and complete reporting project.

Dave, however, simply seemed interested in working on another great story with Nick. He begged to help in any capacity his friend needed. "Throat slitting, drugs, prostitution, phony boobs—all the things I truly love," Dave said. "Nick, please, you gotta let me in on this story. It's going to be another good one, I just know it. What do ya say?"

"I'm heading back up to Mackinac in the morning," Nick said as the two reached Nick's desk in the newsroom. "I'll pick you up at seven thirty. Don't be late or too hung over."

The two friends high-fived, and Dave vacated the newsroom before Clapper knew he'd hitched a ride on Nick's story. It was going to be a wild weekend.

Chapter 6 — Saturday morning

Deputy Delbert T. Pickens, one of Emmet County's finest, adjusted his necktie and clasp in the reflection of his rear passenger's-side window. He tugged up his pants and adjusted his belt buckle so it lined up perfectly with the end of the tie. Symmetry, to Deputy Del, meant everything was in balance and right with the world. When he looked as perfectly proportioned as a honeycomb, he took off his Marine drill instructor–style hat and started working on his mane. The deputy licked the palms of both hands and slicked back the boot-polish-tinted hair on both sides of his head, one strand at a time.

Del tilted his head in both directions in the glass. He whistled appreciatively while putting his cover back on, cocking it slightly to the right—what the ladies told him was his best side. "Lookin' good, lookin' real damn good," he said in a sing-song voice, flashing a toothy smile into the side window. With his index finger he scrubbed away the light film his tongue detected on the outside of his upper row of teeth.

Delbert was so busy preening that he didn't notice the approach of a gold 1972 Firebird—that is, until the driver of the classic muscle car gunned its powerful V-8. The deputy wheeled around to confront the aggressor.

"You almost scared the crap out of me," Deputy Del said, adjusting the gun and utility belt on his hips. He squinted at the two men sitting in the Firebird, a couple of grinning smartass city slickers, he thought. Bright sunlight limited his view. He reached into the breast pocket of his uniform for his mirrored sunglasses. "Oh, okay. There you are."

Nick and Dave waved at the deputy and identified themselves.

Nick thanked him for meeting them at the location where the body of Suzie Alvarez was discovered. They shook hands, and the deputy assured them they could take all the photographs they wanted—he would be happy to point or gesture, or pose for any photo opportunity.

Dave nodded and smiled, taking the hint. He drew out a 35mm camera, set it for auto focus, and then snapped away in Deputy Del's direction.

Meanwhile, Nick surveyed Clatchey Road and the surrounding area. It was barren except for an old Marlette mobile home, which sat in a cluster of trees. Tall weeds and boarded-up windows indicated the trailer was abandoned, ready to fall in on itself. The reporter walked over and peered inside the open door hanging by a single hinge. The ceiling had collapsed onto the floor. Someone had written on the rafters in felt pen: "Edmund Michael nailed this sucker together—summer 1967." It once had housed a family, but now raccoons and field mice were the only inhabitants.

When Nick returned to the vehicles, Dave was informally interviewing Deputy Del about his background. How long had he been with the sheriff's department, he asked, and what did he do for a living before joining law enforcement?

The lawman was happy to share his credentials with Dave, but he was more concerned about what Nick was looking for as he scanned the remote area. Del didn't think he had missed anything during his initial investigation of the scene. But he suspected Nick thought otherwise.

The deputy watched Nick's eyes and tried to answer the reporters' further questions. "Real quiet here, very little road traffic. The lake is in the other direction," he said, pointing north.

No other residences were in sight on this stretch of gravel road, which Ts at U.S. Route 31. The site was south of Paradise Lake and about twelve miles south of Mackinaw City.

The deputy pointed to the side of the road, where the pickup truck with Suzie's body had stalled. Dave stepped sideways and snapped off more photos.

"Whoever was driving just left it sitting here," the deputy said. "Engine had seized—you can see where the oil leaked out before she burned up. Driver took off on foot. We found boot tracks coming from the driver's-side door and heading back up toward the highway."

"Who owns the truck?" Nick asked, moving toward the area where the grass was flattened from the sitting vehicle. "Let me guess. Was it stolen?"

The deputy smiled—good questions coming from a reporter who'd been around the block a time or two. He liked Nick. He couldn't quite figure out Dave, who was suddenly absorbed with photography.

"Yup, old farm truck, which was reported missing from the cherry tree orchards down by Traverse City," Deputy Del said. "Owners didn't know it was missing for more than a week."

Dave asked if he had any leads on the murder case. "I get that the truck quit running, but why was it here?" He snapped off another dozen pictures.

Deputy Del said his department had not received any tips on suspicious activity in the area. He guessed the deceased had been killed somewhere else, buried for a short time, dug back up, and then left on the side of the road when the truck died.

Nick asked how many shovels were found in the truck.

The deputy paused for a minute before answering. He had inventoried the pickup himself, so he knew there were two shovels. That fact might suggest two or more people were in the truck when it quit, but only one set of tracks led away from the vehicle. He had not figured out if the number of shovels was significant, so he wasn't sure he should answer the reporters. How would they use the information, and would giving it to them come back to haunt him? He decided to change the subject.

"Hold on there a minute," he said, turning away from Nick to speak to Dave. "You must have enough photos by now. All that clicking and clacking is making me nervous. Can you give it a rest for a few minutes?"

Dave smiled. He nodded and pulled out his notebook, then scribbled furiously. The deputy cleared his throat and adjusted his gun belt again, this time patting the shiny handcuffs at his hip.

"Shovels? How many shovels?" Nick asked in a quiet voice.

Deputy Del answered by not answering. "It's all in my report, and I'll make sure you get a copy of it." He gave Dave's note-taking a wary glance and moved away from the area where the truck had been found, hoping to wrap up the meeting by asking the reporters if they had any other questions.

The ploy did not work. Nick pushed ahead by asking if the deputy had been offered any assistance on the case. He wondered if state or federal authorities were working with him.

Deputy Del said no assistance was warranted. "Sooner or later, the pieces will fall into place," he said. "These kinds of cases usually solve themselves. Some lowlife will point a finger to get a plea deal, or somebody who knows what happened will shoot their mouth off in a bar."

" 'These kinds of cases?' " Nick leaned against the deputy's shiny cruiser. "What kind of cases?"

"Drug running," the deputy said. "Pretty obvious this was about drugs. Needle marks. She's an illegal. No papers, no identification. Had a couple of tattoos in Spanish and some other marks and injuries. Medical examiner can tell you all about that."

Nick said he and Dave were meeting the ME later in the day. He asked the deputy the same question Dave had asked earlier about the location of the abandoned truck: Why here? What else was in the area?

"Whole lotta nothin'," the deputy said. "Small inland lakes and rivers, some year-round residents and summer cottages. Plenty of woods and empty spaces. Besides that, not much."

Dave pressed him for his thoughts on the case. He asked if the lawman had developed a theory. Where was Suzie being taken?

"Well, they already buried her once," Del said. "My guess is they were looking for a better place to throw her in a hole. You could stick a body in the dirt here, and nobody would have a clue unless a hunter or hiker stumbled across it."

Nick nodded, pausing to absorb the information before continuing. Then why not bury her, he wondered aloud, rather than leave her out in the open in the back of a truck? Wouldn't that make more sense?

"Too close to a main road, and too much time and effort to dig a hole," the deputy replied. "Who would want to get spotted digging a grave with a dead woman nearby? Too risky. I figure the driver panicked and hotfooted it out of the area as fast as he could."

Nick had jotted down everything the deputy said, but he had one more question: how had Suzie Alvarez ended up in a Traverse City funeral home, a hundred miles from where she was found near Paradise Lake?

Couple of reasons, the deputy explained. He had relaxed slightly when the questioning moved away from shovels and on-site planting of the body. "She was unidentified and nobody claimed the body, so we thought this was going to be a county-funded burial. Not many places want to bother with a cheapie. Plus, the funeral director in Traverse City is a brother-in-law of one of our county commissioners. We try to shoot him some business whenever we can."

Nick thanked Deputy Del for his candor. He and Dave jumped back into the gold Firebird, but as they started to pull away, Del raised his hand to get their attention. Nick stopped and rolled down his window to hear what was on his mind.

"From your questions, I get the feeling you don't think we are working very hard to solve this case," the lawman said, leaning down toward Nick's window and into his space. "It's true we don't have much sympathy for druggies, illegal aliens, or gangbangers up here. But I'm doing my best on this case because I got a daughter about this young woman's age—and it was a horrible way for any young girl to die. I'll get it figured out, and I'll make the arrest. You can bet your bottom dollar."

Dave yelled out his window as the Firebird crunched gravel that he would be in touch. Deputy Del's parting comments delighted the reporters, but his actions would mean much more to them than hot air.

Chapter 7 — Saturday morning

As the diesel, 4-wheel drive, green tractor lumbered down Grassmere Road in Huron County, Janene Ortiz kept a close eye on the Chevy pickup that had been following her for two miles now. Juan Perez, the man sitting on the bench seat beside her, asked if it was ICE—US Immigration and Customs Enforcement.

Before she could answer yes, flashing lights and a siren blared from the front grill of the ICE pickup. Janene, her red hair tied back in a ponytail, pulled the tractor over to the side of the gravel road. She and Juan were hauling a ten-thousand-gallon liquid manure tanker to a farm just five miles away.

They both waited in the cab of the diesel, watching for activity in the rearview mirrors. Janene fumbled through her wallet, looking for her license, ownership certificate and insurance. Juan, no different from any other third-generation American citizen, pulled out his driver's license and the miniature laminated birth certificate he always carried with him while traveling across the Thumb.

Janene urged Juan to stay cool—everything would be okay. Cops of any kind, at any time, made him jumpy. She could see the agents advancing, walking on either side of the rig, looking it over slowly as well as under the tanker and between its axles. The outside of the farm vehicle was lightly coated in livestock waste from the tanker's sprayers, making it gooey and stinky, like any manure-spreading machine would be. Janene kept both hands on the steering wheel where they could be seen, but flexed her fingers, telling herself to relax. She took a deep breath and exhaled slowly, letting the warm air from her lungs whoosh through her teeth.

The agent approaching on the passenger's side of the diesel stopped and drew the weapon from his hip holster. The agent on

Janene's side continued walking. She recognized him and rolled down her window.

"Hi, Janene, how you doin' today?" the agent said, smiling as he neared. He studied the monster tractor and peered through the glass of the cab, examining the back area, which was covered with a tarp.

"Excellent, Agent Stevens. Doing fine," she said, forcing a friendly smile.

He asked to see her paperwork. She handed it to him without comment, trying her best to remain calm and seem casual. The tractor was owned by Down Home Dairy Farms, one of the local agricultural operations employing Janene.

Agent Stevens asked about Juan, whom he did not seem to recognize. Janene's companion was ready, handing his documents across her to the agent's waiting hand. Stevens scanned them, then glanced at Juan to see if he matched the photo in the ID.

"Where's home?" the agent asked, looking over Janene's passenger.

"Michigan is my home, Agent Stevens," Juan said, staring straight ahead. "Grew up here, went to school here. Want to see my diploma?"

Agent Stevens grunted. He asked whom Juan worked for and where he slept at night. He cautioned Juan against lying to a federal agent.

"I'm a herdsman. I manage dairy herds, and I work for several farms in the Thumb," he said, agitation creeping into his voice, but he stared straight ahead. "I have a degree in animal science from Michigan State University. My home is in Bay City. My kids go to Bay City Central."

"Well, la-di-da. Looks like we got us a scientist on our hands." Agent Stevens glanced over at his partner, who still had his weapon trained on Janene's vehicle. "Well, we'll see about that. Hang loose right where you are. Don't move. I'll be back."

The agent retreated to his vehicle, which was still running with its grill lights flashing. The fed with the weapon at the rear of the diesel on Juan's side did not move from his position.

Janene spoke in a low voice, looking straight ahead. "This SOB is running a check on you right now," she said. "No outstanding warrants, right?"

"*Sí*," Juan said, his voice barely above a whisper. "I'm clean."

After several minutes, Agent Stevens returned to Janene's window. He thanked them for their patience and returned their papers.

"What are you haulin' back there?" he asked, tilting his head in the direction of the tanker.

Janene studied his face to see if he was kidding. "I could be wrong, but I think it's about ten thousand gallons of cow shit."

The agent smiled. "I know that's a manure tanker, but what have you got in the back of the diesel cab?"

The redhead invited him to take a look for himself. He nodded and walked to the back. The other agent stayed put, keeping a close eye on the two inside the cab.

Agent Stevens peered into the back of the diesel. He lifted the large tarp to see what was under it, then returned to Janene's window.

"All good," he said. "You say you're haulin' cow shit—then you won't mind if we have a little look-see in the tanker?"

"Be my guest," Janene said. "Make sure you cover your nose with a handkerchief when you open the hatch. It's pretty rank."

The agent nodded and used the side ladder to scale the giant triple axle wagon. Once on top, he stepped sideways along a narrow ledge. Janene watched him through her rearview mirror. He covered his nose and mouth with his hat and opened the hatch, examining the inside. His head jerked back. He turned away from the hatch toward the diesel and gagged.

"I think he's going to hurl," Janene said with a grin. She and Juan chuckled quietly, though they did not make any sudden movements in the cab. The other agent still had them covered from Juan's side.

Agent Stevens jumped down from the tanker, not bothering with the ladder. He bent over at the waist, trying to catch his breath. When he approached Janene's side window again, his face was bright red and his eyes watering.

"All good, thanks," he said, his voice ragged and squeaky. He waved them on with his right hand. His left hand still covered his face.

"You bet, Agent Stevens," Janene said. "Any time."

She and Juan continued down the road. In their rearview mirrors, they could see Agent Stevens still bent over and convulsing. The other agent patted his back, trying to comfort him. The sight, and the fact that they had passed another inspection, sparked laughter.

Soon the farm where Janene and Juan were headed came into view. It was another of the Thumb's giant dairy farms, where twenty-five hundred blue-ribbon Holsteins were housed, fed, and milked in a twenty-four-hour production cycle. The Holsteins needed constant care and attention, which meant a significant labor force was required. And providing reliable, cheap labor was Janene's specialty.

The redhead pulled the truck and manure tanker into one of the farm's massive toolsheds. Once safely inside with the doors closed, she and Juan jumped out of the vehicle.

"Hold up for a few minutes," she told Juan. "I want to make sure those agents didn't follow us in here."

Juan nodded, and when she gave him the okay, he tapped the

side of the tanker with a crescent wrench: two quick taps, then a pause, then three taps, then a pause, and four more taps.

Within seconds, a hatch at the bottom of the tanker opened and twenty men crawled out of the sealed, air-cooled compartment inside the manure hauler. The compartment would hold up to twenty-six medium-sized men or thirty women, if they were hunched over and packed in butt to bellybutton. The tanker's top hatch, which Agent Stevens briefly examined, opened to a two-foot-deep container that ran the length of the tanker. It held about five hundred gallons of liquid manure.

The men who had rolled out of the tanker stretched and spoke among themselves in Spanish. Juan motioned for them to follow him to a corner of the toolshed. He pushed a hay wagon away from the corner and moved a half-dozen cement blocks, then opened a door in the floor. That led to a secret basement, complete with bunk beds, a gang bathroom and shower, a full kitchen, and an office with two MacBook Pros and a snazzy color printer.

Juan showed the newcomers their temporary accommodations. Then Janene laid out the rules: no alcohol, no drugs, no women, no fighting. "And clean up your own damn mess, including the bathroom and shower, every damn day."

She asked if they had questions. One man wanted to know how they would pay for their living expenses.

Janene held up a large hardcover book. "This is my bible," she said. "Each and every one of you has an account in this book. I keep track of all your expenses—from the food you eat to the water you drink to the clothes on your back. Those expenses and the costs to handle them are deducted from the pay you get every month. You have any problems whatsoever, you let Juan know. If he can't fix it, he will bring it to me."

Juan translated and the men murmured quietly. Janene and Juan searched their eyes to see how the arrangement she'd described settled with them. They both asked if the men had any more questions. For the moment, they did not.

"All right, guys, you can stretch your backs out and loosen up by shoveling shit this afternoon," she said. "We got two hundred calf pens that need cleaning. Let's get busy."

Juan translated Janene's commands, and the twenty men were led back up to the toolshed. The redhead watched them head off to work for the day. Then she jumped back into the diesel truck and towed the manure tanker to another site to transport more laborers. So much work to be done, so few workers to accomplish it all.

Chapter 8 — Saturday afternoon

Soon after Nick turned onto I-75 heading north, he could tell that Dave was laboring. Rapid, jagged breathing. Cold sweat. Eyes darting. Knees bouncing up and down like the cylinders in the Firebird. Finally his friend implored him to stop the vehicle, or he would be sick to his stomach within a few minutes.

With his finger shaking like a leaf on a tree, Dave pointed to the Mackinac Bridge, looming gigantic, bad, and bold a few miles ahead. Nick nodded and looked for a safe place to pull over on the side of the freeway. The last thing he wanted was somebody vomiting in his precious Firebird.

Once the vehicle rolled to a stop, Dave hopped out and crawled into the back seat. He stretched out and asked his friend for a blanket. Nick retrieved a large gold-and-green blanket with "WSU" — Wayne State University — printed on each side. He tossed it to his friend, who grunted his thanks and covered his shoulders and head.

"Go ahead now. Please turn the radio on and don't talk to me," Dave said, his voice muffled under the blanket. "And whatever you do, do *not* describe what you see when you're driving over the bridge. Just let me know when we're safely on the other side."

Dave was not alone in his fear of heights and of crossing Mighty Mac — the Mackinac Bridge — which spans five miles connecting the Upper and Lower Peninsulas of Michigan. The bridge is one of the longest expansion bridges in the world and stands a full two hundred feet above Lake Michigan.

The drive across the bridge produces stunning views of both peninsulas but can also turn stomachs into rumbling, churning washing machines for those who have a condition known as gephyrophobia.

Every year, more than a thousand people call the Mackinac Bridge Authority, asking about the Driver's Assistance Program, which offers motorists a driver to get them across the bridge—in either direction—if they cannot manage it themselves.

The height of the bridge did not bother Nick. In fact, he had walked the bridge several times during the governor's annual Labor Day bridge walk. In Nick's view, it was an invigorating experience, and he looked forward to the trek by vehicle or foot whenever he could fit it into his schedule.

But on this day, he and Dave were working. They were on their way to visit the medical examiner in St. Ignace, who handled autopsies for rural Emmet County when needed. It wasn't a pleasure trip—not that this was ever a pleasure for Dave.

As Nick approached the bridge, he felt the Firebird's gradual ascent and could hear Dave's breathing escalate at the same time. Dave stayed under the blanket, repeating over and over, "I'm not going to die today. I'm not going to die today. I'm not going to die today." Dave's voice rose one octave at a time as they moved up the bridge.

By the time they hit the apex, Nick could have sworn he had a teenager squealing in the back seat. But soon they were on their way down, descending to the UP side of the bridge, and Dave's chants slowed and became less shrill. He flipped off the blanket in time to watch the Firebird roll back onto firm, stable roadway.

Nick was glad St. Ignace was only seven miles from the base of the bridge. He did not want to stop again so Dave could move back up to the front seat.

"We'll be at the doc's office in a few minutes," he said, glancing into his rearview mirror to check on his partner. Dave was staring back through the Firebird's rear window, examining the bridge as it shrank in size. "Are you okay now? You're not going to hurl, are you?"

Dave moaned but did not turn around and face Nick. In the distance the bridge became smaller and smaller. "How long before we get there?" he asked.

Dave's voice was so soft that Nick thought he might actually be introspective. He wondered if his friend had another problem he didn't know how to handle. "Are we going to have to look for a place for you to change underwear?"

"Who says I'm wearing underwear?"

Nick laughed. His friend was fine.

They turned into the parking lot of the St. Ignace Medical Clinic, then rolled out of the Firebird and stretched. A receptionist greeted them at the front door.

"We're here to see Dr. Rossini," Nick said, identifying himself and Dave. "We have an appointment."

The receptionist asked them to take a seat while she alerted the doc. It was a small waiting area, only eight chairs in the place, and half of them were filled with folks who looked like they needed care, not the services of an ME. Dave indicated he was going to look for a restroom.

While he was gone, Nick checked out the degrees and certificates posted prominently on the walls. Dr. Rossini had graduated from Central Michigan University. He had become a Doctor of Osteopathy at Michigan State University. The paper on the wall also indicated he had studied forensic science at Wayne State University. He wondered if the doc had trained under the famed Dr. Werner Spitz.

The receptionist was back within ten minutes to tell Nick Dr. Rossini was running late but would make it to the clinic shortly. He had asked the receptionist to seat the reporters in his office. Dave returned in time to be led into the doc's office, which was spacious and dominated by a desk and adjoining worktable covered in mounds of reports and files.

As soon as the receptionist left the room, Dave started pawing through the files on the doctor's worktable.

"You know those are confidential," Nick said, pointing at the stacks of paperwork. "If the doc comes in and sees you looking through medical files, we'll be kicked out of here before we even have a chance to ask a question."

"Well, he's not here yet, and judging by my experience with doctors keeping their appointments, I figure we got at least a half hour before he shows." Dave moved to another stack of files and continued to dig. "Why don't you go stand by the door to slow down the receptionist or doc if they do come in?"

Nick did not want to be an accomplice, but he was also curious what Dave was turning up. "Anything good?" he asked.

Dave hesitated while he scanned the outside of a new file. "Oh, not much. How about a file labeled 'Jane Doe/Alvarez'?"

Nick leaped out of his chair and was by Dave's side as the reporter opened the file. It was the autopsy, including ten pages of notes and photographs.

Dave offered to watch the door while Nick took photos of the report with his cell phone. They moved quickly, and within seconds Nick had finished capturing images of each page of the report, whose contents stunned the reporters. Not only had Suzie's skull been crushed and then her throat cut, but scars on her back and buttocks indicated she had been whipped on at least two different occasions. Suzie also had needle marks in her armpits and between her toes and fingers.

"Drugs," Nick said, flipping to the next page. "Maybe that's it, maybe this is all about drugs—like Deputy Del said. Like some in the newsroom said. Man, if this all boils down to drugs and fulfills the stereotypes, that would really tick me off."

Dave shook his head. "I got my doubts. I think Deputy Del would have trouble finding his way out of bed in the morning. I wonder if the ME filled Monica in on the extent of the injuries."

The office door swung open, sending a rush of air through the office. The reporters scrambled to put the file back together and slide it into the stack where they had found it.

Dr. Rossini was not fooled. He sat in his chair and kicked his feet up on the desk, crossing them at the ankles. "I'm not supposed to let you see that file," he said. "Too bad I left it on the desk instead of securing it."

Nick looked at Dave, who smiled ear to ear. Nick asked why the ME had left it out for them.

"That poor woman was tortured," the doc said. "The injuries to her ankles and wrists tell me she had been chained up, and more than once. She was beaten, probably with a whip or some kind of electrical cord. Looks like she may have been drugged too. Did you notice in the photos that her pinky fingers were broken? Somebody needs to do something about this, but my job will be done when I get the drug analysis back from the lab. I was hoping you guys would pick it up."

Dave asked about local law enforcement. How had the cops reacted to a report showing pretty clearly that a young woman had been tortured before her violent death?

The doc threw his hands in the air, palms up. Local police agencies were stretched thin by budget cuts, he said, and northern Michigan was one of the poorest regions in the country. Every government agency struggled to stay on top of the basics—even law enforcement had trouble meeting the needs of the people who lived in the area and paid their salaries. Police had their hands full with crime that ranged from trespassing and poaching to theft and drugs to assault and rape to all forms of domestic violence.

"Let's face it," the doc said. "This woman was not local, and nobody is screaming for the crime to be solved. How many people in Emmet County, or anyone up here, give a damn about this poor, unlucky foreigner? Not many. If your newspaper shines a light on it, maybe it will get solved and we'll find out what's really going on here. It's gotta be bigger than what happened to this poor kid. The only ray of light among the local police is Deputy Pickens. He's a good cop who cares—just overwhelmed like everybody else."

Nick nodded and confessed to taking cellphone images of the autopsy report.

The doc did not seem surprised. "You didn't get them from me, and I have no idea how you acquired them."

He told the reporters he would help in any way he could—on condition that he not be quoted directly or as the original source of information, such as the autopsy report.

Once back in the Firebird, Nick pointed the machine in the direction of Bay City. Both reporters were excited by what they had learned from the ME. They were eager to share it with the C-Man and continue their investigation.

For now, though, they were nearing Mighty Mac. Dave dove into the back seat and looked for his blankey.

Chapter 9 — Saturday night

Tanya Johnson stepped out from the front door of O'Hare's Bar & Grill and looked in both directions down Midland Street for the Firebird. No sign of Nick and Dave.

Where were the guys? Fearing the worst, she wheeled around and marched back inside the bar to join her friend, Jennifer Walker, a former schoolmate in Bay City and at the University of Michigan. They shared a love for Chardonnay, premium chocolate, romantic black-and-white movies from the 1930s and 1940s, and education.

Growing up, the two girls were never far apart. Some thought they were related, cousins or sisters—they even dressed alike. Today they both wore blue jeans, high heels, and pastel sweaters.

Jennifer had met Nick two years before during a social event organized by Bay City schools to raise money for underprivileged children. Tanya had set up tonight's meeting because Jennifer knew of an educator in the Thumb who might help him with the Suzie Alvarez story.

"I hope they didn't stop at a bar on the way home," Tanya said. She checked her cell for the time again and sipped her wine.

Jennifer placed a hand on her friend's arm. "Nick and Dave stop at a bar? Why, I'd be shocked," she said, laughing loudly enough for people at the next table to notice. "The better questions might be, Will they make it home tonight, and will Nick be wearing pants?"

They both roared at the comment. But Tanya pushed back, saying that Nick had not really lost his pants because they were hanging from the ceiling at O'Hare's—a few feet from them now.

Jennifer did not back away. She asked about the incident at the Mustang Lounge on Mackinac Island. "Didn't I hear something about beer euchre and shamrock shorts?"

Tanya was surprised that her friend had heard about the wild drinking episode. But before she could respond, the front door of the pub opened and Nick and Dave walked in, both appearing to be sober and fully clothed.

The reporters spotted the women and approached their table. Nick gave Tanya a hug and kiss on the cheek. Dave greeted Jennifer by saying hello and offering his hand for a shake.

"No way," she said. "I don't know where that hand has been today, and to be quite frank, I'd be afraid to ask."

"Frank? I thought you were Jennifer. My mistake," Dave said, reigniting the long-running strife he had with Tanya's friend. Neither of them cared much for the other. To her, Dave was crude and uncouth. To him, she was snooty and pretentious.

Dave turned his attention to Tanya, complimenting her on a new hairstyle. He pulled a stool up to the table and waved at Sassy Sally behind the bar, circling an index finger in the air to request fresh drinks.

"That was a long, dusty road down from Mackinaw City," he said. "We are parched and ready for some brews."

"Really? Did you and Nick walk all the way back?" Jennifer said.

Nick grimaced at the comment. Jennifer and Dave could not help being snarky with each other, but Nick wanted to head off the tit-for-tat conflict. He and Dave had picked up some great information in St. Ignace, and Nick didn't want their progress derailed by verbal war between two friends.

"So, Jennifer, Tanya tells me you might have a contact for me," he said. "Tell us what you know."

Jennifer said she had worked with a woman employed by the Huron Intermediate School District who oversaw a minority educational outreach program, designed to help the children of migrant workers stay on top of their schoolwork.

The educator often worked with Catholic Family Services to help the poorest of the poor, Jennifer said. "They know the farms and they know the people. They try really hard to keep track of what's happening with migrant workers, hoping to stop them from being taken advantage of or abused."

Nick pulled his notebook out of his jacket pocket, opened it to a blank page, and handed it to Jennifer. He asked her to jot down names and contact info.

As she did, Tanya reached under the table and grabbed Nick's hand. She squeezed and held it tight while letting it rest on his knee. Tanya leaned over and whispered in Nick's ear, so close her lips brushed the back of his ear, "Love you, and glad you're back."

Though they'd talked by cell, the couple had not spent any real time together in days. The physical distance bothered both of them, but their crazy, time-devouring careers kept the two on the run. They savored the chance to be together, even when it meant sharing with friends.

"Okay, okay, you two. Break it up over there, will ya," Dave said. "If you keep going, I may have to look around here and find me a barfly."

Jennifer could not resist the opening Dave left her. "That shouldn't be a problem. Flies are always buzzing around you."

She pushed the notebook back to Nick. The open page had two names on it—Torrey Van Dyke and Sister Sharon—plus two cellphone numbers.

"You'll love the nun. She's a sweetheart and a hoot. Everybody in the Thumb calls her Sister S.," Jennifer said, raising her wine glass to her nose and sniffing before pressing it to her lips for a sip. "Torrey is very officious and a stickler for detail. They're a good combination."

Tanya added that she had known Sister S. for years through St. Boniface Catholic Church in Bay City. The church brought nuns in to teach catechism on Saturdays to kids who didn't go to Catholic schools.

"She knows how to use a ruler to keep your attention," Tanya said, rubbing the back of her hands. "Jennifer had class with her too. She made it a point to keep the thirteen- and fourteen-year-old boys away from us all afternoon long."

Nick thanked Jennifer and said he would try to call them Sunday to see if they could meet on Monday. He hoped the two women would be able to provide behind-the-scenes insight into migrant life on the dairy farms. They also might be able to take him and Monica physically inside that life and introduce them to people who had known or worked with Suzie Alvarez. He knew Monica would be enthused to meet folks who could help them retrace Suzie's steps during the last year.

Nick told Tanya and Jennifer about the intense initial encounter with Suzie's sister in Traverse City. He recounted how Monica was crushed after learning what had become of her sister, and her brutal death, but told them she was committed to finding out the truth. Monica would be in Bay City Monday morning to continue the search for answers.

"She seems like a real tough cookie," he said. "She's thankful for our help but says she's going to get the truth regardless—no matter how long it takes."

Dave told the women about meeting Deputy Del. He said the guy seemed more interested in getting his photo taken for publication than finding out what happened to Suzie. The deputy had assumed Suzie's death was drug related, and the reporters were not convinced that law enforcement was interested in investigating the case.

Tanya asked why the deputy assumed Suzie's death was connected to drugs. "Did the cops find drugs when they discovered her body?"

Dave shook his head no. "They didn't actually find drugs at the scene, but there were indications of drug use."

Nick broke into the discussion. He did not want to reveal too much about what they had learned, especially the information that was confidential or had not been verified. He would give Tanya details when they were alone. The reporter lifted his draft beer and swallowed the contents in three gulps, leaving white foam on the edge of his silver mustache. His darting tongue did the work of a napkin.

The others took their cue and finished their drinks. Dave wanted to order more, but Tanya put the brakes on that idea like a dragster near the end of a quarter mile.

"You can if you like, but Nick and I are going to his place," she said. The conviction in her voice left little room for doubt. Nick did not argue either.

Dave faced his buddy with pleading eyes. "You used to be such a fun guy. Sure you don't want to stay out and have some fun— maybe hit a few places, carouse a little, and start breaking stuff up until they kick us out?"

Nick smiled and pulled Tanya close. "It sounds like I'm going to have some fun at home instead. Maybe I'll catch up to you Sunday afternoon."

Tanya shook her head decidedly. "Nick, remember, we're taking mother to Mass in the morning. You promised. No fun tonight. Early to bed, early to rise."

Dave could hardly believe what he had just heard. His old friend had become domesticated as a household pet. Taking his girlfriend's mother to church on Sunday morning was certainly a step toward the altar. "Well, that's right, Nick, old buddy," he said. "Be a good boy tonight. The only guy with blurry eyes and wine on his breath in the morning better be Father O'Reilly."

Nick laughed and shook his head, heading for the front door of O'Hare's. Jennifer and Tanya gave each other a long, firm hug. Dave was the only one to keep his seat.

Chapter 10 - Sunday afternoon

Monica Alvarez pulled her cousin Hector in close for a hug. She tucked an envelope with four hundred dollars—all twenties and fifties—in his jacket pocket, all the cash she could spare to get Suzie home. Monica urged him to drive safely and asked him to call her when he arrived in Mexico.

Earlier, she and Hector had gone through the pile of documents she had compiled to make Suzie's exit from Michigan legal. She had cautioned Hector to obey all traffic signs and speed limits. It was imperative that he not get pulled over by police while traveling. Monica prayed all would go as planned so she could give her sister a final, dignified farewell.

"I trust you, Hector," she said, wiping tears from her eyes with a sopping hanky. "Take Suzie home and put her to rest. I'm staying here for as long as it takes to find justice."

Hector nodded and gave Monica's hand a final squeeze. Then he climbed into the van and drove away. Monica watched until the van and her beloved sister disappeared from sight. She took a deep breath and exhaled.

The funeral director called to her from the front door of the funeral parlor, asking her to come into his office to sign some final documents. Plus, Monica thought, he would have the bill for Suzie's arrangements ready. He had agreed to take care of her sister and help complete all her paperwork for the base rate of eight hundred dollars.

Monica was grateful for the accommodation. While he had initially been a bit stiff and formal, the mortician had become kind and gentle while getting Suzie ready for transport. She sensed he was genuinely moved by her sister's brutal murder.

Monica walked back to the park where she'd met with Nick, and sat at a picnic table in the shade of a tall oak tree. The breeze off Lake Michigan was stiff today but warm. Watching the lake was almost hypnotic to her. She closed her eyes and smiled as a fond memory of Suzie came to mind: the days when they both were youngsters playing in the backyard of their small home.

The game was hide and seek. It was their favorite, though most of the hiding places were no longer secret. Monica would count to twenty while Suzie dashed for cover. They would chase each other and laugh for hours. It was a game and ritual she would never forget.

"Oh, Suzie, Suzie, I miss you so," Monica said out loud. Tears filled her eyes as she searched her pockets for more tissue. "You were always so stubborn. What in the world did you get yourself into? And why did it cost you your life?"

The girls had remained close through their teens. When they lost their parents to a house fire, their bond heightened. After their brother joined the Marines in San Diego, the young women parted to pursue professional careers and their dreams of managing world-class resorts. Monica took an internship with an international hotel chain in Acapulco. Suzie chased her dream to Mackinac Island. The sisters stayed in touch by cell, text, and email while they built their resumes. But communication between the two slowed and then stopped altogether within weeks after Suzie lost her job and work visa.

Monica blew her nose hard and blinked away what was left of her tears. How Suzie had ended up in the back of a pickup truck was a mystery, but she knew in her heart that it would not stay that way for long.

Nick had arranged accommodations for her in Bay City through

Our Lady of Guadalupe Catholic Church, which served most of the community's Hispanic population. Parishioners were outraged when they learned what had happened to Suzie Alvarez. The Garcia family was one of several that had volunteered to help Monica; they said she could stay as long as she needed.

Monica was grateful for the support. Chasing down Suzie's killers would be a monumental task, but she pinned her hopes on Nick Steele, a man she believed would not rest until they uncovered the truth.

Chapter 11 — Sunday night

Juan Perez fumbled with the settings on the printer in the business office of the toolshed basement. A sign above the doorway to the office declared its name and purpose: "Documents A-Go-Go."

Juan leaned into the machine and moved the color rollers back slightly, hoping to improve the efficiency of the reproduction equipment. He cursed softly in Spanish, as if that would solve the problem.

Juan was Janene Ortiz's fixer of all things big or small, a man who could get to the root of anything difficult and solve any problem. He and Janene had worked together for more than a decade. Over the years, he had proven himself time and again, and Janene trusted him implicitly. She could always rely on him.

He felt the same way about her. Janene had saved him when he first arrived in Michigan as a teenager with nothing. No immigration documents, no money, no work prospects, and no skills. Like thousands of others, he had come here riding a rickety raft made of dreams and hope.

Janene, ten years his senior, saw a bright bundle of raw energy. She took him under her wing and trained him. Additionally, he was big, strong, and handsome in a rough, Charles Bronson sort of way, and as time passed, the two became intimate. When Janene needed a strong, calloused hand, she would call on Juan to satisfy her needs. He was honored that she trusted him to take care of her most private fantasies. Juan answered her call every time, without reservation.

They made a good team. And they made a lot of money. Janene trusted Juan to oversee half the labor camps on the eastern side of Michigan. He rotated between the camps, handling emergencies among workers and the farmers they worked for. As a native

Mexican, he also helped Janene gain the trust of the people she managed.

Juan plugged the machine into the wall outlet, and it roared back to life with the ring of a bell and a continuous hum. Now it was time to test it. Juan clicked the print button on his MacBook Pro. In seconds, a birth certificate rolled off the printer: a male named Pablo Sanchez, born in Botsford, Pennsylvania, in 1983.

Juan held the bonded paper up to the fluorescent light overhead and moved the document up and down, back and forth, to view it from different angles. The Great Seal of the Commonwealth of Pennsylvania marked the top of the page. It featured a bald eagle, a ship under full sail, a plow, and three sheaves of wheat. He wanted it to be just right.

"Here, take a look at this and tell me what you think," he said to Chico, who was pecking away on another MacBook Pro in the office. The man started to reply in Spanish, but Juan held up his hand. "No, say it in English. You must practice to wear off the hard edges of your accent."

"Looks good," he said, turning to Juan for approval.

"Full sentence. Practice speaking in full sentences," Juan said. "If you are going out in public, you need to get the language down. You don't want to sound like you just swam across the Rio Grande."

"The certificate you are holding looks very good," Chico said, pronouncing each word. He smiled when he finished and glanced at Juan again for approval.

Juan nodded. He was pleased with Chico's English and the quality of the birth certificate. It mirrored the real Pennsylvania birth certificate that Juan had saved on his computer screen. He clicked another button that commanded the printer to spit out nine copies. Within seconds, he had documentation for ten men born in Botsford in 1983, each named Pablo Sanchez. The certificates would go out to new arrivals, undocumented laborers, in ten secret migrant camps across Michigan.

The quality was as good as the diploma he had made for himself from MSU's agricultural school. Juan had never finished high school and did not have any advanced education, despite what he boasted to law enforcement and anyone who listened to his lies and exaggerations. The only thing he knew about animal husbandry was that he had to get a bull and heifer together to create a calf, and he hadn't learned that in a classroom.

Chico waved for Juan to check out the MacBook's screen, which displayed a Social Security card with the name Pablo Sanchez. The Social Security numbers had been purchased off the internet, harvested from the accounts of dead people. The numbers were real but inactive. They would not remain that way for long.

Juan reached across Chico and clicked the button to print out the card. The printer, which was the size of a steel filing cabinet, was a technological marvel that could do just about everything but fry eggs in the morning. Sure enough, Pablo Sanchez's Social Security card passed muster, so Chico printed nine more.

"What else are you working on?" Juan asked. He pushed back the thick, curly dark hair that had fallen forward as he hunched over Chico's machine.

Chico handed him a diploma from Mayville High School dated June 1, 2001. The graduate: Pablo Sanchez.

"Mayville? Where did you pick up on that?" Juan asked, holding the diploma up to the light. "Has anybody worth a damn ever graduated from Mayville?"

"One of the slugs who operates the big field machinery, the combines, is from Mayville," Chico said. "I heard him talking about it, so I dug up a diploma online and copied its seal, design, and logo. I thought it was cool—just another piece of ID one of our *amigos* can use if they get pulled over by the cops."

Juan nodded but corrected Chico again—English only.

"Yes, sir," Chico replied, and printed out nine copies of the diploma.

As they watched the high-tech machine spit out its work, Juan turned to his understudy. "Hey, Chico. Want to graduate from Harvard? It won't take four years. I can take care of it in four minutes."

The two men laughed and high-fived.

Chapter 12 - Monday morning

Nick stood at the front door of the *Bay City Blade* with two copies of the paper carrying his front-page stories about Suzie Alvarez. He had promised them to Monica, who he expected to arrive any moment. Nick had invited her to the newspaper because he wanted her to meet the C-Man, Drayton Clapper.

Precisely at eight o'clock, Monica walked through the front door, where Nick greeted her with the day's paper. She looked beyond him into the wide-open circulation and advertising departments just past the entrance to the newspaper. The offices were coming alive with loud conversation over a backdrop of ringing telephones and copy machines chugging away.

They walked past the offices, attracting stares from the men and women who came from all walks of life to form the *Blade* team. Monica was a striking woman, and Nick was always bringing someone interesting into the *Blade* building. That combination made tongues wag in a lot of different ways today.

As they walked up the stairway to the second floor and the *Blade* newsroom, Nick prepped Monica for the meeting with the C-Man. "Now, sometimes Drayton comes across as kind of a hard-ass, but he's a good journalist and a fair and fine man. If my buddy Dave is not in the newsroom, then we'll have a fairly good chance of catching the C-Man in a good mood."

They did not.

The newsroom was in chaos, and for good reason. The Bay City teachers union, which had been threatening to strike for weeks, had selected that morning to put teachers on picket lines and shut down the schools. This, of course, meant that thousands of parents in town were unexpectedly without their paid daily daycare services for offspring aged five to eighteen.

Clapper spotted Nick and Monica at the entrance to the newsroom and waved them over to his office. They whisked past reporters working their telephones and computers at the same time. Editors huddled nearby, plotting coverage strategy. Photographers hunted for a place to download their images—picket lines, protest signs, and teachers marching and chanting the very same hackneyed clichés they chastised their students for using.

The meeting with the C-Man was short and to the point. Clapper, to Nick's amazement, turned on the charm. He shook Monica's hand with both of his massive meat hooks, left one on top, patting the top of her hand softly. "I'm so sorry about your sister. Please offer my deepest sympathies to your whole family. Nick has told me about you. You are welcome here, but we have a bit of a crisis on our hands this morning, so I have to run pretty soon."

Monica tugged gently, then withdrew her hand from his grasp by jerking her elbow backward. But she smiled and thanked him for the welcome. "I know you're busy, but I'm glad we met," she said. "I am here with one purpose, and that is to find out who killed my sister. I want the truth—whatever it is. I am hopeful you can help me find it."

"That's what we're after too," Drayton said. "Nick's a good reporter. He knows what to do, and we'll be in constant contact. We will decide what, if anything, is published—I can make no promises to you. But we will chase this story wherever it goes."

Nick and Monica hustled out of the newsroom, leaving reporters and copy editors whispering in their wake. Nick knew there would be a faction who might work against him while he was out chasing the story. For now, Dave would keep his ear to the ground in the newsroom.

As the two made their way down the staircase to the front entry-way, Monica noticed a sign that had been taped to the inside of a clear plastic cubicle in the newspaper's circulation department. In big, bold all-caps letters was a racial slur and the words "go home."

Nick stopped to see what had caught Monica's attention. His blood boiled—with rage and embarrassment. He apologized to Monica and escorted her to the front door, then ran back to the cubicle and yanked the sign down. The occupant of the cubicle was stunned. He remained silent while Nick wadded the sign up and tossed it in the trash. Every member of the department had stopped what they were doing to watch the reporter.

Nick leaned into the cubicle. "You are a total asshole. I am ashamed that anyone in our organization would do such a thing. I got my eye on you."

Monica was waiting for Nick at the front door. He apologized again, but she brushed aside the slur.

"It doesn't bother me, Nick," she said. "And it's not just your newspaper. I've been experiencing that kind of attitude and hate since I arrived. Don't get me wrong—most people I've dealt with have been kind and friendly, but I hear or see that sort of thing almost every day."

Monica smiled and turned her back on the *Blade* building, putting the slur and the person who wrote it behind her. "Really, I don't care right now. We're on a mission to find justice for my sister, and I can put up with ignorance and intolerance as long as it doesn't get in my way. Let's get going."

They were scheduled to meet Torrey Van Dyke, the county educator Jennifer Walker had recommended, in Bad Axe. Nick told Monica they were likely to be on the run all day. He offered to drive them to the Thumb.

As they drove east on Center Avenue, Monica marveled at the

historic Victorian homes lining both sides of a four-mile stretch. Nick watched her gaze dart from one massive three-story house to another. He began his standard three-minute Center Avenue history pitch, "It all started with lumber …"

Before he could finish, he noticed Monica poking around in her purse. Finally she got right to the point and asked for an update on Suzie. She wondered what Nick had discovered in just a few days of inquiry.

Nick asked how much she wanted to know—as he and Dave had learned from Doc Rossini, it wasn't pretty.

"What did you get from the funeral director and the ME?" Nick asked, stealing a quick look at Monica to gauge her reaction. He accelerated as they left Essexville and moved into the countryside. "I can tell you what I found out, but I don't know how much you really want to know."

"I want the truth, Nick. I'll tell you when it's too much."

The reporter nodded and scanned the traffic ahead on M-25. Nick feared the horror of Suzie's final days might be too much for Monica to handle. He wanted to help, not hurt her more. He asked if she knew how Suzie died.

She replied calmly but looked out her side window and not at Nick. "Blunt object to the side of her head," she said. "Just below the temple." Then she added, "Throat slit to make sure the job was done."

Nick was relieved to hear her unemotional response. He took it as a signal that it was okay to give her details, even if they were gruesome. He asked if Monica had been apprised of Suzie's injuries. Did she know about the other trauma to her body, some occurring months before her death?

"He didn't say and I didn't ask, but I do want to know." She stared straight ahead at the bright blue sky across a horizon of flat farmland. "What injuries?"

"A finger on each hand had been broken and healed." Nick pulled the Firebird out into the oncoming lane to pass a monster combine. "The ME said he thought they had been broken at the same time."

"Oh … my … God, torture," she said, the words firing from her mouth. "They tortured her, Nick. The bastards. Don't tell me any more. That's enough."

For several minutes, the two did not talk. Nick focused on the road while Monica, her head down, fumbled with the wad of tissue in her lap.

"Which fingers?" she asked.

Nick hesitated, not sure exactly how to answer.

"Which fingers, Nick?"

"The pinky on each hand."

"Oh, not the pinky fingers! If you want to truly hurt a laborer, you damage their tools, their hands. That would hurt like hell. Those bastards!"

The reporter stopped at the main intersection in Unionville and pointed the Firebird toward Sebewaing. Monica wanted more information. "What other injuries?" she asked.

Nick avoided the question by turning the discussion to their surroundings. The community bulletin board, he noted, boasted of an upcoming soup supper as a fundraiser for a family burned out of their home. Nick thought that would make a great column, and the soup created by a bunch of German grandmothers could not be topped.

"I don't give a damn about soup," Monica said, slamming her open right hand on top of the purse in her lap. She turned to face the reporter directly. "What other injuries, Nick?"

"Suzie had been beaten on two different occasions," he said, glancing over at Monica.

"What do you mean, beaten?"

"Struck with a cord or a lash of some kind," he said. "The first assault was five strokes, and the second, a couple months later, ten."

"Oh my God, they whipped my sister. Those sons of bitches," she said, now openly sobbing. "My dear, dear Suzie, whipped like a dog. Worse than a dog—nobody would hurt a dog like that. Oh … my … God, Nick. No more. Don't tell me anything else. I can't take it."

They drove in silence for several more minutes. Nick stopped at Sebewaing's only stoplight and turned right toward Bad Axe. But once they cleared town, Monica picked up the conversation again, asking Nick if there was more.

Nick did not want to give her the final detail, but he was afraid it would come out as they tracked Suzie's trail. He decided to blurt it out.

"Drugs. The ME said he found evidence—needle marks between her fingers and toes and in her armpits—that she was on heavy-duty drugs, heroin, crack," he said, watching the road ahead. He could feel Monica's stare like a heat lamp on the side of his face and neck.

"Oh … my … God. They got her hooked on drugs. Those lowlife animals," she said, the words coming out in a slow whine. "How could they, my sweet Suzie? She would never take up drugs on her own. Nick, I told you not to tell me. How could you tell me?" Monica leaned forward, forearms on the dashboard, and buried her face, her back heaving as she cried her heart out.

Nick was speechless. He had feared that the graphic details would be too much for her, and now he wished she had not pushed him so hard. Monica looked so distraught that he wondered if they should turn back and call off the day's meetings and interviews.

Within a few minutes, Monica started to rebound. First, the wailing and sobbing slowed. She wiped her eyes and blew her nose. Two deep breaths, and Nick could see her shoulders lift, her chin pointed up and straight ahead.

"That's why we have to see this through," she said, determination steeling her voice. "The cruelty and barbarism cannot be let go. I am more committed than ever to finding out everything—and I mean *everything*—that happened to Suzie. I owe it to her and will not rest until the guilty are caught and tried for their crimes. Are you with me, Nick?"

Nick relaxed in his seat. Monica was back on her game and ready to go. He wanted to reassure her.

"Just like the C-Man said. We are going to chase the truth wherever it takes us," he said, catching a quick glimpse of his passenger. "Now, let's go talk to some people who might help us get answers."

Monica wiped her eyes again and smiled. Nick pushed the Firebird toward Bad Axe. He was thirsty for hot coffee and fresh information.

Chapter 13 — Monday morning

The late-morning crowd at Coffee Cup Plus, located kitty-corner from the courthouse, near United Title Company and two blocks from the *Huron Daily Tribune*, gulped hot, steamy brew and swapped stories. Lawyers, realtors, and journalists—among the least-trusted professionals in America—always gathered at this little oasis. They had lots of information to share, some of it even based on facts.

Nick and Monica wriggled through the mob in the coffee shop and found an empty table in a corner. Before they could plant their bottoms in the seats, Torrey Van Dyke approached and introduced herself.

"Hi, Nick, Monica. I knew it had to be you because you're the only strangers in here," she said, a friendly smile spreading across her round face. Her brown hair was cut short and combed back with a natural part at the very top of her head. She looked stout, but in her case, the bathroom scale would say appearances are often deceiving. Torrey stuck out her hand, and Nick grabbed it before handing it off to Monica.

"Glad to meet you," Nick said, returning the smile. "Heard a lot about you from Jennifer."

Monica focused on Torrey like an owl zeroing in on a titmouse. She studied her every move and devoured each word she spoke, not saying a thing herself, watching and nodding.

Nick jumped up to get coffee, leaving the women to talk. Torrey started by offering her condolences to Monica for the loss of her sister. She said she had learned of the tragedy from Jennifer.

"Well, that's why Nick and I are here," Monica said, making heavy eye contact with the woman. "We want to retrace her steps in the

Thumb and learn what happened to her. Jennifer says you are very well connected out here."

Nick returned to the table with three Columbian coffees and a giant sticky bun on a paper plate, cut three ways. Napkins spilled from the breast pocket of his dark sports jacket. He spread the goodies in the center of the table, and each of them reached for a cup.

Torrey said they would need one more coffee in a few minutes. She had invited another woman to join them—a nun with Catholic Family Services Outreach, an area mission dedicated to helping the poor. Sister Sharon could add valuable background to their discussion, she said. That was good news for Nick and Monica, who had been enthusiastic to meet the nun since Jennifer mentioned her.

Monica stirred a splash of cream into her cup. She picked up where she'd left off with Torrey, not wasting a moment on small talk. She asked if Torrey knew of a woman in the Thumb named Janene who hired people to work the farms.

Torrey nodded. "Janene is kind of legendary or even mythical out here, known of but rarely seen. I'm curious how you came onto the name—gossip or solid information?" she asked.

Nick said he'd heard about Janene from Ned, the charter boat captain he had met up at Mackinac Island. "Ned said Janene paid for Suzie's transport to Port Austin. Said she also took care of Suzie's tab, probably room and board, on the island. But Ned said he didn't have a last name or contact for Janene." Nick sipped his coffee, then used a butter knife to trim off a corner of the sticky bun.

"Ah, yes, Ned, the creepy, smelly sea captain from Grindstone City," Torrey said. "He's a pretty wild character in his own right. They say he will do about anything for cash. Lots of whispers about him. He's the kind of guy who would know Janene."

"Says they've never met, which I'm not sure I believe," Nick said, licking his index finger and thumb clean of gooey sugar. "So, tell us about Janene. Do you know her last name?"

Monica listened intently, sipping her coffee. She did not pick at the pastry.

Torrey casually glanced over her shoulder in each direction. Coffee Cup Plus was said to have more ripe and ready ears than a Huron County cornfield. No one looked their way. "She goes by Janene Ortiz, but who knows if that's her real name," she said. "I have my doubts—she's a very shady character. What we do know is that she works for many of the big dairy farmers across the Thumb. She bills herself as a labor consultant and contracts separately with the big operations."

"So, she's legit?" Nick asked, stirring his coffee again. "She's under contract with the farms?"

"Well, that's the big mystery. Nobody knows how it all works. My understanding is that she gets paid a set fee from the farmers," Torrey said. "But there is a lot of talk about Janene also getting paid tons of cash—all under the table—to supply labor, which she in turn pays five bucks an hour."

Monica asked what kind of work her sister might have done if she had been employed by Janene. She wondered how many laborers this Ortiz woman managed.

Before Torrey could respond, a woman in a modern nun's habit, a cowl fashioned from a navy-blue wrap, a short black scapula, and a powder-blue skirt covering the knee, glided to their table. Sister S. stood short and thin, fuzzy gray hair poking out from the sides of her cowl. She wore wire-rimmed granny glasses and had rosy red cheeks and lips that did not require the aid of makeup. No one would have doubted that she was a nun.

The three stood to greet Sister S., but she could not take her eyes off Monica. "JESUS, Mary, and Joseph!" she blurted, making the sign of the cross with her right hand. "You look just like Suzie.

In fact, I thought you were Suzie when I first walked in."

The nun's words hit Monica like an uppercut from a boxer. Her eyes widened and her jaw fell open, but no words came out for several moments.

"You knew my Suzie?" she said, her hands rising. "Oh my God. Please tell me everything about her."

Sister S. pulled Monica to her shoulder and gave her a gentle hug. Monica started to weep. "I'm so sorry, child. I'm sorry you lost your sister."

Nick and Torrey remained standing, witnesses to the tender moment. They said nothing as the older woman comforted the younger one, still obviously in mourning. She patted Monica gently on the back.

Torrey announced she had a business meeting to attend and would have to leave. She and Nick exchanged business cards, and she gave him a scrap of paper with a name and an address. "We're meeting a dairy farmer at two today," she said. "Don't be late."

Nick looked at the paper and nodded. Monica and the nun broke free from one another to say goodbye to Torrey, who suggested that Nick and Monica ask Sister S. about the labor camps. Then she hustled for the front door.

"The labor camps—that's where I met your sister about a year ago," the nun said, pulling her chair closer to the table. "She and a few other women were at a farm raising heifer calves. The women had their own small barracks away from the main barn and homestead."

Sister S. said Suzie seemed to be doing well except that her pinky fingers had been injured and were bandaged with popsicle sticks as splints. Monica stiffened at the nun's remarks but relaxed as she continued by saying that Suzie looked thin but did not complain.

Nick, enthused to learn more about the overall operation, asked about the labor camps that Torrey had referred to. He wanted to know how many existed and where they were located.

The nun held up her hand, trying to slow Nick down. She had heard reports that as many as a dozen labor camps were operating on a wide range of farms, from Saginaw to the west all the way to Harbor Beach on the east side of the Thumb.

"All told, we might have five hundred undocumented workers in the area," Sister S. said. "But Janene is probably the only person in the whole region who knows how many are here, and that's because she's the one who brings 'em here and moves them out."

The number surprised Nick. He asked Sister S. how she came up with it and if she had been to all the camps.

"Nobody knows how big the operation is or how many people are involved," she said. "It's a cradle-to-grave system Janene runs. She takes care of all the workers' needs— food, clothing, transportation, money transfers, mail, laundry, documentation—for a fee, and it's a stiff fee. Some of the laborers never get caught up."

"Sounds like sharecropping to me, or another form of slavery," Monica said, drumming her fingers on the table. "We've heard reports that workers are sometimes shackled and beaten. Are they locked up at night? Is that true?"

"I've not witnessed shackles or beatings, but I have seen Janene walking around with a whip dangling from her belt. JESUS, Mary, and Joseph," she blurted, once again making the sign of the cross with her right fingers tapping her forehead, chest, and each shoulder. "She is evil, and the cinders of hell will one day sear her black soul.

"They let me bring the blessed sacrament of communion to a few of the very secluded camps on Sunday afternoons. It gives me a chance to check on them and make sure they're all right. But it only gives me a snapshot of what their lives are like."

Monica asked if they could visit the calf-raising operation where-Suzie had worked. She wanted to know if any of the women there still remembered her sister.

"I might be able to take you on Tuesday, but I'll have to make sure it's okay for you to visit," the nun said. She did not want to take strangers to the property when farm managers were present. They usually inspected the operation on Mondays.

Nick was delighted. But before he could reply, he heard a voice call out on the other side of the coffee shop, "Hey, Booger, you going to the big game Friday night?" Nick's ears pricked up. He scanned the room and spotted J.R. Ratchett, Huron County sheriff's deputy, sitting with jailhouse employees at a large, round table.

The reporter popped out of his chair and rushed over to the deputy's table. Ratchett, better known as Jay-Bob, saw him coming and rose, a grin spreading across his face.

"Well, what in the gol-durned heck are you doing here again?" Jay-Bob asked, his right hand outstretched for Nick to grab. He teased the reporter by cautioning the folks at his table, "Hey, everybody, watch what you say—we got us a big-shot reporter in the house."

Nick laughed as he and Jay-Bob shook. He told the deputy he was working on a new story that was tough to crack—and he could use some help. The deputy nodded and asked what Nick needed.

"If you wanted to get the skinny on undocumented workers in the area, who would you talk to?" Nick said. "Who has their finger on the pulse of illegal immigration?"

"Why, that's an easy one," Booger said, rubbing the side of his nose and resisting the almost overwhelming urge to pick it. "Ice ice baby! You got to talk with ICE Agent Phillip J. Stevens. He knows everything there is to know about undocumented people out here. Why, he's out chasing 'em across the Thumb every day."

Nick asked for a cell phone number, which Jay-Bob scratched onto a napkin. He said he would call the agent and tell him to expect a call from Nick.

"Phil owes me a big favor," the deputy said. "I know he'll give you a hand, but he's sometimes hard to pin down. Give him a call, drop my name. Tell 'im you got Booger on your hands."

Nick fought off the urge to laugh and thanked the deputy. He returned to his table in time to say goodbye to Sister S., who had another meeting to attend. She said she would call Monica when she was able to arrange a visit to the calf-raising operation. Monica thanked her and excused herself to use the restroom.

The nun seemed in a hurry to leave, but she pulled Nick aside, standing on her tiptoes to speak into his ear. "Others have gone missing. Suzie is not the only one."

Nick recoiled at the news. He studied the nun, trying to gauge the expression on her face.

"Over the last ten years, I've noticed a number of laborers in the camps disappearing," she said, moving in closer to Nick again. "At first, I didn't think much about it. But then a pattern emerged, especially among the women. They were working, trying to start a life, and then they were gone. Nobody would say where they went or what became of them."

Could they have transferred out of the area? Nick asked. He sat back down at the table and urged the nun to join him—even if it was only for a few minutes. She did.

"Transfers were different," she said, crossing her arms on the table so that her chin was only a few inches above them. She leaned close to Nick, her voice barely above a whisper. "The people who went somewhere else to work—well, we would hear through the grapevine how they were doing. Little tidbits here and there. Sometimes they would send cell phone photos or a special note on a birthday. But that wasn't the case with those we started calling 'goners.' If I asked Juan what became of so-and-so, he would dismiss my question by saying they'd moved on, then change the subject. After a while, I started keeping a log."

"How many disappeared?" Nick asked, his voice as soft as flannel. The two were inches apart.

The nun held up her right hand and flashed five fingers once, then twice.

"Five? Five people disappeared over ten years?"

"No, fifty-five," she said, her voice barely above a whisper. Nick thought her cheeks were getting rosier the more she talked about these so-called goners. "Double nickels. I made a spreadsheet. Names, ages, how long they worked here, and when they disappeared."

But the nun hadn't reported the disappearances. "Who would I report it to?" she said. "How do you report the disappearance of someone who is not supposed to be here? Who would back up my story? Nobody. And I'd be putting myself in trouble, maybe even harm's way. Juan is a bad man. I don't trust him."

Nick asked if he could see the spreadsheet and copy it. He said he didn't know how he might use the info, but it might be useful as this story unfolded.

Sister S. nodded as she stood to leave. "I'll get it for you, but now I'm really running late. Gotta go."

The nun floated out of the shop, the ends of her cowl and long skirt flowing behind her, just as she had entered.

Chapter 14 — Monday afternoon

Nick and Monica watched the long line of cows flowing into the milking parlor at the McDonald Farm in southern Huron County. The line would never stop. The milking operation ran continuously. Cows went in and got washed down, milking machines were attached to their udders, and they came out and went back to feeding, then returned for a second milking at the other end of the day.

Nick had grown up on a farm in the Thumb, so the pungent aroma from the barnyard did not incapacitate him. But Monica, who had never visited such a big dairy farm, had to cover her nose and mouth with a hanky. Even so, she whispered to Nick that she felt like gagging.

Nick urged her to breathe slowly and allow her senses to adjust. If that didn't work, he asked her not to vomit on their hosts—the farm manager and Torrey Van Dyke. She nodded, her eyes streaming.

Bud Raffendale, who had been a farmer his entire life and managed dairy operations at the McDonald Farm, explained the process to his visitors. Bud was an imposing figure. He was dressed in blue jeans from head to toe: jean jacket, shirt, pants, and hat. He stood about six feet tall and carried a beer drinker's potbelly and matching rear end. A two-day growth of brown stubble covered the bottom half of his cheeks and chins. A smile never seemed to leave his face, even when he frowned.

The milking went on 'round the clock, Blue Jean Man said, but so did the feeding and the waste removal. With hundreds, sometimes thousands of twenty-five-hundred-pound animals, it was a big job.

"Of course we have all the modern equipment, but it also takes a ton of labor, which must work 'round the clock too," he said. Bud reached into his jean shirt pocket and withdrew a long, thin cigar. He stuck it into the side of his right cheek and rolled it around with his teeth. "Problem is, I don't know of anybody from West Bloomfield or Rochester Hills who wants to come up here and take a backbreaking job for low pay."

Monica asked why the laborers didn't get more pay and benefits. Torrey was ready to answer the question, but Bud replied with a question of his own.

"Do you know anybody who wants to pay twenty-five bucks for a quart of ice cream? How about twenty bucks for a gallon of milk? People in this country have become accustomed to plenty of fresh, cheap food. They expect it and wail like wounded animals if prices go up—even a few pennies. Our grocery stores and food production and delivery systems are the envy of the world. So, how do you change a system that's so efficient?"

Torrey tried to offer perspective. Cheap labor was in high demand all across the state, she said, not only on dairy farms. The latest Michigan Department of Labor statistics showed that at any given time, about forty thousand undocumented laborers lived and worked in Michigan. Many were employed in agriculture, but they could be found working across most industries, from convenience stores to building and road construction contractors to hotels, restaurants, and bars.

"In many cases, they're taking the jobs no one else wants to do for low pay," she said. "They live and work in the shadows. What a lot of people don't understand is that we have work that needs to get done. Nobody wants the grunt work, the dirty jobs."

Bud moved the cigar, still unlit because of the highly flammable hay and straw nearby, to his other cheek and rolled it between his teeth again. He offered to take his visitors inside the milking parlor to watch the operation close up. Nick was all for it, but the women were not. Monica was struggling to keep her composure and her breakfast.

Instead, she asked Bud if the McDonald Farm used undocumented laborers. He did not think so, he said: all prospective employees must produce papers that proved citizenship or legal status. Hiring required an extensive screening process.

"But sometimes the paperwork we're given looks so authentic that we don't realize it's not until they've been here awhile or until they get arrested. If they get into trouble, then all hell breaks loose," he said, nodding in the direction of a group of men loading feed for the animals. "ICE agents stop here pretty regular to check our books, count heads, and survey the property. We do our best to operate within the law. I know some of the big dairy operations are not as thorough as we are—lots of stories out there—but we've never been cited."

Nick reached into the inside breast pocket of his jacket for Suzie's photograph. He asked Bud if he recognized her. The man studied the photo and moved it sideways into the sunlight, then eyeballed Monica. Then the picture again.

"Pretty girl. Gotta be your sister," he said. "No, can't say I've ever seen her in these parts. Is she missing?"

Monica said yes, her face grim. She explained how Suzie's body had been found in northern Michigan—and how they were trying to find out what became of her by retracing her steps, which had led them to the Thumb and the dairy farms.

Nick could see that the photo and Monica's words had hit home with the farmer. He felt like the timing was right to drop the bombshell. He asked Bud if he knew of a woman named Janene who worked for some of the farmers in the Thumb.

Bud's ever-present smile faded. "I know of her—almost everybody up here does," he said, withdrawing the cigar from his cheek and spewing a stream of brown juice on the ground about ten feet from Nick. "She is bad news—mean as a snake and has a wicked bite. We don't deal with her. I've been instructed by the farm owner not to allow her on the property or work with her in any way."

Monica said they had learned that her sister was working for Janene. She wondered if Bud knew where they might find the notorious labor consultant. He shook his head no, saying he rarely ran across her. Blue Jean Man shifted his weight between his feet, almost swaying side to side.

Nick thought he seemed uncomfortable. He also noticed that Bud's right cheek twitched while they talked about Janene. He wondered if Bud was holding back information or stretching the truth. The farmer seemed edgy, almost nervous.

"She's got red hair, tall and thin, pretty hard to miss when you see her," Bud said. "But she stays on the move. I know ICE agents are always on her trail. They track her like bloodhounds, but I don't think they catch up to her much. She's a pretty smart cookie, from what I hear."

Blue Jean Man put the cigar back in his mouth and moved it from side to side, presumably with his tongue. He offered his visitors a tour of the feeding stations and storage barns. Again Nick wanted to nurture his curious soul and take the tour, but the women declined. Torrey had another afternoon appointment, and Monica was fearful she would become ill.

On their way back to Bay City, Monica sat in silence as the Firebird rumbled through the vast, flat farm fields of the Thumb. Normally she was talkative and generally upbeat. Now her eyes were downcast, her shoulders drooping. Her fingers rolled the hanky in her hands. Nick tried to lift her spirits.

"I thought we had a pretty good day," he said, glancing between the road and the woman in the bucket seat beside him. "Lots of good information. I have a better understanding of how this all works and the great demand for labor."

Monica gazed out her side window, waiting a few minutes before responding. When she did, her voice was not filled with optimism. "Yes, it was good, but we are no closer today to finding out what happened to Suzie than we were three days ago," she said. "I had this feeling while we were talking to Bud that this is going nowhere. That, and the god-awful smell, kind of overwhelmed me."

Nick, almost always a force of positive energy, tried to offer her words of encouragement. He had traveled the road of inquiry and discovery many times—it was always a long, hard journey. Good journalists knew they had to stay positive, keep moving, and continue to claw for the truth. He shifted his left hand to the steering wheel and leaned on the center console, moving closer to Monica.

"I know this can be frustrating. Digging out information is often a slow, tedious process," he said. "But really, we're just getting started. If we keep working at it, we might catch a break and the whole thing will come spilling out. Hang in there."

Monica turned to face Nick and smiled. She said she would do her best to remain patient.

Billowing smoke from the Karn/Weadock power generating plant rose into the sky against the horizon. As the outskirts of Bay City came into view, they discussed their plan for the next day. While they were still at the farm, Monica had received a text message from the nun. They were set to meet Sister S. and visit one of the farms where Suzie had lived and worked.

"I've also got a call in to the chief ICE agent in the area," Nick said. "He's going to meet with us, just doesn't know when yet. We'll work that in as it comes up."

The Firebird motored into the South End of Bay City, where the Garcias lived just off Broadway. It did not look as though anyone was home. But the family had hidden a key in an outside birdfeeder, Monica said. She asked Nick to wait a moment because she had something for him in the car. He watched as she opened the trunk of her rental and rummaged through the contents.

"I picked this up for you in Traverse City," she said, motioning for him to come over to the vehicle. "Just a little something for all you are doing for our family." Monica pulled a folded wool blanket out from the mess, and a brown cardboard box fell to the ground. It was labeled "Jane Doe/Alvarez."

Nick held up the blanket to the light: slate gray with large yellow and maroon stripes. A tag in the corner indicated it came from the Traverse Bay Woolen Company, which meant it was a quality weave. The reporter was delighted. He thanked her for the thoughtful gift and folded it over his left arm.

Monica picked up the box, and a shirt spilled out from its side, revealing a dark-brown stain on the collar. Nick recognized the remnants of dried blood. He asked about it.

"These are Suzie's things—what she was wearing when they found her," she said, trying to poke the shirt back into the box. "It's all I have left."

The reporter was shocked she had evidence pertinent to Suzie's death. Normally the authorities would never let evidence out of their possession—unless they didn't believe they had a case.

"How did you get your hands on it?" he asked, examining the box and drooling to get his hands on its contents himself.

Monica pursed her lips. She did not make eye contact with Nick, keeping her peepers trained on the box in her hands. "I promised not to tell. I don't want to get anyone in trouble. Let's just say I ended up waiting a long time in the medical examiner's office waiting for him to keep his appointment with me."

Nick smiled in understanding. "But that evidence might have come in handy when the killer or killers are caught," he said, his voice rising. He feared a significant blunder had occurred. "Now that it's fallen out of police possession, it's spoiled. No judge would ever let it come back into the case."

"I understand," Monica said, and she raised her eyes to meet Nick's again. "But I had nothing left from Suzie's life. This is a treasure to me. I spent an hour with the ME's secretary. She knew what I was going through because she had lost a brother in a hunting accident. When I left, I had the box."

Nick didn't say anything. He watched her pull the box against her chest, wrapping both arms around it in a bear hug.

Then she continued. "The secretary said I might as well take the box because it would end up gathering dust in an Emmet County evidence room. Nick, she told me flat out not to count on anything coming from an investigation because everyone in the sheriff's department was swamped with real cases. Can you believe it? She said 'real cases.' Nobody would give Suzie's death a second's notice. No time for drug addicts, gangbangers, or foreigners, I guess."

Monica did not cry, but Nick thought she was close to bursting. He wasn't quite sure how to comfort her. What words would ease her pain? What gesture could take the cruel sting out of the secretary's words? He stood by her side in silence a few moments, then finally asked if she had examined the clothing.

"Did you go through the pockets? The cops would do that routinely, but sometimes they miss things," he said, eager to do the task himself but not wanting to upset Monica by acting too aggressive, especially with something that had her sister's blood on it.

Monica said she had looked it over when she received it. The only thing that had come out of the pockets was dirt, probably from when Suzie had initially been buried.

Nick wanted to check but decided not to push it. He thanked Monica again for the gift and said he would see her Tuesday morning after he checked in at the *Blade* newsroom.

Chapter 15 — Monday evening

Nick opened the front door to his apartment building, and Jenni, the exuberant black lab belonging to his landlord, leaped up and stuck her front paws on his chest. The dog tried to lick the reporter's face too, but Nick held her off, promising a biscuit from his apartment.

The dog's tail smacked against the wall as she followed him to his door. Once inside, Nick grabbed a goodie from the dish in the entryway and flipped it into the air. Jenni leaped as high as a fat lab could and snapped it up.

"Nick, is that you?" Mrs. Babcock, his landlord, called from her apartment on the first floor. "Send Jenni downstairs when you get tired of her slobbering and drooling on your floor."

"I will, but I was hoping to talk to you," he hollered into the cavernous hallway, his voice echoing. "Can I bother you for a few minutes?"

Mrs. Babcock urged him to come down to her place. Bring the dog, she said, and two cold beers.

Nick shot to his bedroom and changed out of his basic reporter's uniform—sports jacket, button-down collared shirt with loosened necktie, slacks that kinda matched, and hard-soled shoes, which he examined closely for remnants of cow manure. He did not believe he had stepped in dung during the visit, but anything was possible on a farm.

While he donned jeans and a pullover shirt, Jenni watched patiently from the bed, where she was sprawled out against the pillows.

Nick stepped into his sneakers and opened the top drawer to his dresser. He rummaged around for the small box hidden there and stuck it into the back pocket of his jeans.

Then he grabbed a couple bottles of ice-cold Labatt from the refrigerator and headed for the door, the dog moving in sync with him as if they were part of a Marine Corps drill team.

Mrs. Babcock's door was open when Jenni reached the bottom of the stairwell. A recording from The Moody Blues played in the background. Nick ditched his shoes on the square of carpet to the side of the doorway and set the beers on her coffee table. Mrs. Babcock was nowhere in sight, but he didn't let that slow him and Jenni down.

In the kitchen he found frosted mugs—and the remnants of homemade meatloaf in a pan on the stove. Nick hacked off a chunk and gobbled it quickly enough to make Jenni jealous—not only because he got the treat but also because he wolfed it down like an animal.

"You'll find some cold glasses in the freezer," Mrs. Babcock called from her bedroom. "I'll be right out."

Nick sat on the couch in her living room to pour the beers, and just as the last drop hit the thick layer of foam on top, Mrs. Babcock entered the room wearing a full-length light-blue housecoat adorned with yellow flowers. Bunny slippers and white socks covered her feet. Her graying sandy hair was rolled up in fat, round curlers, and the bump in the middle of her long, thin nose kept her black-rimmed glasses from sliding off her face.

Mrs. Babcock grabbed a mug and swallowed two large gulps of the golden liquid. She licked her lips. "Boy, is that good. Thanks, Nick. I was ready for that."

The reporter raised his glass. "Mrs. Babcock, you've got to toast before you start guzzling the stuff down."

She laughed, and they clinked glasses. "Here's to the new story you're working on. May you have continued success and catch the dirty bastards who took the life of that young woman."

"Couldn't agree more," Nick said. He tipped up his beer and watched Mrs. Babcock intently, always curious about how his landlord viewed his work. "I was wondering how you would react to the stories we've published about Suzie. Did I tell you I'm working with her sister, Monica?"

His neighbor shook her head no as she placed her mug on the table. A small burp, almost inaudible, escaped her lips, which had formed a perfect O. Nick recapped what they had discovered the past few days. He said he liked Monica and hoped he could help her solve the mystery surrounding the death of her sister. But he also believed the story was becoming much bigger than the tragic, brutal death of a single woman. Suzie Alvarez, he said, was simply the tip of the proverbial iceberg.

Mrs. Babcock took another sip. She asked Nick if he wanted her opinion on the matter, but before he could respond, she offered her thoughts, which was completely in character for his never-bashful landlord.

"If Suzie hadn't been breaking the law, she'd probably still be alive," she said. "That may sound harsh, but the girl was here illegally. Sounds like she was dabbling in the underbelly too, the underground, involved with people who live off the charts. That's always dangerous."

The woman continued, her curlers bobbing and her voice growing bolder. Immigrants built this nation, she said, with her ancestors coming here legally from England and Ireland. "My, oh my, they had it tough," she said, staring out the apartment window at the backyard and alley, where a stray cat picked at garbage that had seeped from a plastic bag. Nick could tell by the disdain on her face that the scavenger distressed her. "They worked from sunup to way past sundown. I read a passage in our family Bible about it. My grandmother took in washing as a third job—that was the only way they could eat every day."

Nick watched his friend carefully as she talked. He thought he saw her tremble as she brought old family memories back, which triggered memories of his own—stories of his ancestors' origins. They were alike in two ways: Though the immigrant's journey in America was tough, it was far better than the conditions they had left. And their hopes and dreams had carried them through their ordeals.

"You're right, Mrs. Babcock," Nick said, patting Jenni on the head and rubbing her ears. The pooch gave a low moan. "If she had returned to Mexico after losing her job on Mackinac Island, she might be alive today. But she didn't, and now we are dealing with the reality of what happened to her—and believe me, it's not pretty. Certainly she didn't deserve to die."

The landlord drained her mug and asked Nick if that was what he'd wanted to talk about. Nick said yes, then reddened slightly and shifted in his seat, becoming coy or almost shy. "Well … there's one more thing I wanted to discuss."

The reporter reached into the back pocket of his jeans and pulled out the small blue velvet box, which he nudged across the coffee table. Jenni focused on the box and drooled, as if it might have a pork chop in it.

Mrs. Babcock studied the box for a moment. Her eyes lit up at the diamond ring inside. "Aw, Nick. I wish you hadn't done that. You know I'm too old for you," she said, beaming with pride and wriggling in her seat. "Can you return it and get your money back?"

"Ah, Mrs. Babcock, the ring is for Tanya," he said, not sure if his landlord was serious about the gift being for her. "I'm planning to propose one night this week. Wanted to see what you thought about it."

"Ha-ha, of course it's for her," she said, examining the ring again with a hint of sadness in her expression. "It's lovely, and Tanya will be so excited."

Nick said he was afraid Tanya would reject him. Deep down, he believed he was not worthy of her. He had plenty of flaws—probably a workaholic who poured all his energy, time, and skills into his job, and a problem drinker, perhaps even an alcoholic if past wild episodes were any indication. Plus, he did not think he was her equal intellectually. He was a reporter with a BA from Wayne State. She was a highly regarded educator with enough degrees and certifications from U of M in Ann Arbor to paper the walls of her apartment. He had served in the Marines overseas. She had studied abroad summers during college. He had grown up on a farm in the Thumb while she had lived her whole life in the city. To Nick, a good time was cold beers with friends at O'Hare's. Tanya enjoyed sipping wine at a reception before an evening at the symphony.

Two people who loved each other very much but were very different in so many ways. Nick wondered if a life together would work for them—was love enough? But he had concluded Tanya would not wait for him forever, and he did not want to risk losing her. If he was going to give them a shot, he believed it had to be now. Nevertheless, self-doubt haunted him: Would she say yes or laugh him out of the room?

Nick was delighted that Mrs. Babcock, at least, hadn't burst out laughing when he told her the ring was for Tanya. "She could do so much better than me," he said, gesturing with his hands like he was conducting an orchestra. He rattled on, having explored every aspect of their relationship repeatedly in his mind. "I'm not in her league. She's so smart, a real intellectual. And funny. And pretty. She has a big heart, and she's a dozen years younger than me. She has no flaws."

"Well, that's a load of crap," Mrs. Babcock said. "Everybody has flaws. You're just so mesmerized by her right now that you don't see them. But you will."

Mrs. Babcock grabbed the two empty beer mugs and stood, a signal to Jenni and Nick that she was almost ready to retire for the night. "That girl would be absolutely crazy to say no. Now that you're in control of your drinking, you're a darned good catch for anyone. Don't worry, she won't turn you down. If she does, let me know and I will slap some sense into her."

The two friends laughed and talked for another hour before Nick jumped up from his seat to leave. He had another big day ahead in the Thumb with Monica.

Chapter 16 — Monday evening

Juan checked his cell phone for the time. No messages yet. He and Janene had waited in the Auburn Hills mall parking lot all afternoon in their van for the arrival of their cargo—thirty-seven undocumented laborers coming to metro Detroit from just outside Columbus, Ohio.

"No calls, emails, or texts," he said, shifting in the seat in a futile attempt to find comfort. "I'm going into the store to use the can. I've got to move around some."

Janene nodded. She planned to do the same thing as soon as he returned. He was twitchy, and it was making Janene more nervous than she already was.

They had not worked with this dealer before, and now her mind raced with apprehension. Had ICE agents intercepted the truck? she wondered. Had state or county cops pulled over the driver? Could the transporter have had mechanical problems? Had a difficulty occurred with the cargo? Had the driver become ill?

Janene scanned the parking lot, which looked big enough to contain several football fields. Moms pushed shopping carts overflowing with purchases and kids. Young people chatted and texted as they headed for their vehicles. Men pulled supply carts from the furniture outlet in the mall. But no refrigerated truck came into sight.

The redhead turned her attention to the van's radio for a distraction and some lively music. The search button stopped on an oldies soul station where the DJ had cued up "My Girl," by Detroit's own Temptations. The sweet melody and harmonies brought a smile to her face, and Janene relaxed a bit, her senses coming down a few notches from high alert.

"My Girl" was the song her second husband, Armando Ortiz, sang to her before he proposed. Though the proposal had come twenty-three years ago, she remembered it as if it were yesterday. Without question, the night of their engagement was the happiest time of their relationship.

Two years after they married, Armando, a hot-tempered alcoholic, killed a man with a broken whiskey bottle in a bar fight. The man had spilled the whiskey, and Armando, in a booze-fueled haze, figured the guy should pay for the mistake with his life. But the next day he couldn't recall the battle, which bar patrons described as epic and messy. He awoke to the prodding of a San Antonio police officer's steel-cased flashlight.

The killing brought Armando a twenty-year jail sentence. Janene waved goodbye to him from the courtroom as deputies dragged him away in wrist and ankle shackles. She then walked down the hall of the courthouse and filed for divorce. Armando had beaten her at least once a week since their three-day honeymoon. When her husband was arrested, she had been looking for a way to escape. The judge and jury made it easier for her.

With Armando out of the picture, Janene launched what would later become her labor consulting business. Texas was <u>full of undocumented migrants</u> frantic to find their way north to almost any kind of work. The redhead, a native of Michigan, was fluent in Spanish and identified a service industry niche she could fill. She would connect desperate immigrants with businesses that were equally desperate for labor. The best part was that it paid handsomely.

The song ended, and Janene hit seek. A modern rap number by a would-be poet with an indistinguishable name followed on the airwaves. Janene hit the seek button again and looked up in time to see Juan emerge from the store, carrying two bottles of water and a sack of sandwiches and fries so greasy they had already soaked through the bag.

As Juan settled back into his seat, one of the cell phones rang, causing them both to jump in their seats. They looked at each other, their eyes as big as saucers. Janene handed the blaring cell to Juan because this was his new talent supplier.

He clicked the phone on. "What the hell is the problem? We have been waiting for hours." Janene could hear panic in the Spanish reply on the cell. Juan's expression soured, as if he had been punched in the gut. He clicked off without saying goodbye.

"A problem came up—a big one," he said, looking out his side window, avoiding eye contact with Janene. "We're in the wrong place, and it's the wrong day. The shipment came yesterday."

Juan started the van and the two drove in silence to a mall in Troy, some twenty miles away in rush-hour traffic. They spotted the truck sitting alone in the farthest corner of the parking lot. Juan drove up to the truck and surveyed the scene around them, making sure no one appeared interested in the refrigerated truck or their van. Still without speaking, he got out of the van and climbed the steps to the cab, peering inside. The driver was long gone. The passenger's-side door was open. Juan stepped inside.

The cab was empty. Keys to the ignition were on a chain on the floor. The truck was not running, though, and neither was the small diesel that ran the cooling and ventilation system for the truck. The truck was loaded with vegetables and fruit, but false walls inside created a sealed compartment for human cargo. That compartment was locked from the outside and could only be accessed from inside the cab. Juan and Janene had seen the truck used for shipping laborers once before, and it had worked without flaw, keeping the veggies, fruit, and humans all cool and fresh for successful delivery.

But not this time. When Juan opened the door and stepped out of the cab, his left hand covered his nose and mouth. Janene could see the horror in his eyes. Her worst fears were realized.

"They're all dead," he said, gasping for air as he slid back into the van. "Gone. All of them. Suffocated. I could see where they had clawed the doorway to get out. They shit themselves. It's horrid."

"Damn you, Juan! Damn you to hell." Janene lunged across the console to swing at Juan with both hands, her voice harsh and pointed. "You put this together and you screwed up. Now we've got dead bodies and blood on our hands. Damn you, Juan, you killed those people. We're going to prison, and then we're both going to hell."

"Shut up, bitch. I got this," he said, scanning the parking lot again to see if anyone was watching. "I'll fix it."

Janene didn't shut up. Juan pushed her away and raised his right hand in the air, showing her the back of his big paw. Within seconds, it was clear that was a mistake.

"Don't you ever raise your hand to me," she bellowed. "I found you pulling weeds in a bean field, and I can put you back there any-time I want. You ever raise your hand to me again, I will rip that arm out of its socket and jam it where the sun don't shine."

They both leaned back in their seats and breathed heavily. Janene was already figuring their next move. They were sitting in a corner of a monster mall in metro Detroit next to a truck with thirty-seven dead Mexicans decaying in a hidden compartment. Now what?

Janene's mind raced. She had been hoping to retire soon and leave the business to Juan—maybe another year or so of peddling flesh, then move to the little villa she'd already purchased in Argentina, a country that once welcomed Nazis and laughs off most attempts at extradition. But now she feared this horrible incident—thirty-seven dead—could ruin them and destroy everything they had built. If they were discovered, they'd have the full weight of the law down upon them.

And the deaths brought other problems that had to be solved.

How would they replace the workers who were already scheduled for jobs on farms? How would this be explained to the farmers? How would it be explained to the people who had shipped the cargo? Who would pay for the loss? How would they get rid of that many bodies all at once? What would they do with this big-ass truck that was now permeated with the smell of death?

"Janene!" Juan burst into her thoughts. He said he would drive the truck north, but he wanted her to follow him in the van. As long as they didn't get pulled over for inspection, he said, they would be okay.

"No speeding, use turn signals, no rolling stops, go easy." His words broke off as he tried to get his breathing under control. "Don't do anything stupid, and we'll make it."

They didn't have much choice. What else could they do, she thought, call for road service? Nobody was going to help them. They had to get out of this mess themselves. She agreed and hoped her nerves would not betray her as they drove out of the city, though she felt as though her head was swiveling like Linda Blair's in *The Exorcist*—fitting for the evil she was now a party to. She thought about the panic, fear, and agony of those trapped inside the truck during their final hours. She cursed Juan again and again, asking how he could have messed up the exchange so badly that they now had more blood on their hands.

Janene followed Juan out of the parking lot and onto I-75. Just ahead she could see the Palace at Auburn Hills. They both drove sixty miles an hour in the far right lane—nice and easy. Soon they would be out of the metro area, heading north. Dusk was falling around them like a curtain coming down on a bad act. She took a deep breath and relaxed as traffic thinned.

Juan had said he could fix this. Janene prayed that he was right.

Chapter 17 — Tuesday morning

Nick rushed into the newsroom, hoping he could make his visit a quick stop. Drayton Clapper had asked him to come by the office before returning to the Thumb—Morton Reynolds, the *Blade* editor, wanted to meet as soon as possible.

The C-Man was huddled with copy editors when Nick made it to the newsroom. He checked for messages but found only two, one from Dave and another from a source he was working with on a city hall story. Both could wait. Nick filled out an expense account form, stapled a dozen receipts to it, and dropped it on Clapper's desk while the editor was distracted. The reporter was running low on cash and hoped to be reimbursed—quickly.

When the C-Man finished talking with the copy desk, he motioned for Nick to follow him to Reynolds's office on the third floor of the *Blade* building. Nick started for the stairs, but the C-Man pointed at the elevator.

Clapper said he had an idea what Reynolds wanted to talk about, but he hoped he was wrong. He did not say any more.

Nick wondered what he had done to warrant a face-to-face confab with the Worm, the nickname newsroom staffers had tacked onto the paper's spineless editor. "Let me guess," he said in a quiet voice. "Are advertisers complaining about our coverage of the Suzie Alvarez story?"

The C-Man did not respond. His gaze remained focused on his shoes, his expression dour. Nick took that to mean he was right. He said nothing else.

The only noise was the moaning and creaking of the elevator as it lurched upward. When the doors opened, Nick stepped out as fast as he could. For years he'd feared getting trapped in the elevator—

especially with the publisher, Diane Givens, known far and wide as the Castrator.

The C-Man followed Nick out and led the way into Reynolds's office. The editor, an avid fly fisherman, sat behind his desk reading *Field & Stream* magazine. He chuckled to himself as his guests took seats in front of the desk. Must be a cartoon with short words and large print, Nick thought.

"Gentlemen, please come in and take a seat," Reynolds said without looking up, gesturing toward the fat-cushioned chairs in front of his cluttered desk—after they had already seated themselves. "This shouldn't take too long. I wanted to make sure we were on the same page with the story you're working on, Nick."

"What page would that be?" Nick said, settling back into the cushy seat in search of comfort that would not be found.

The C-Man did the same thing but held his hand up, fearful Nick would become agitated before he knew exactly what was on the editor's mind. "Let's hear Morton out, Nick. We may be thinking the same thing."

The editor cleared his throat. He tapped a notebook with the ink pen in his right hand. The tapping made all three men uncomfortable, but Reynolds did not stop until he spoke.

"Let's talk about where we are going with the Suzie Alvarez story," he said, his voice low and calm. "You've done some good work with it, Nick, but it may be time to go in another direction. I'm not sure the subject matter is worth the time and energy we're putting into the story."

Nick's pulse raced, his anger rising. Silence, at least for the moment, he thought, was his best option. The reporter could see concern in Clapper's eyes, and he trusted the C-Man to make their case for chasing the story.

"Morton, we're making great progress on the Alvarez story,"

Drayton said. He shuffled his ample behind farther back into the chair, causing the cushion to exhale with a whoosh. "We need to keep pushing. It's bigger than we thought—we don't know how big yet."

Nick nodded in agreement and checked Reynolds's face to see if the C-Man was winning the moment. The sour look on the *Blade* editor's scrunched-up face told Nick that either the man was having some serious heartburn or he didn't like what Clapper was saying. Pressure, Nick thought, from outside forces had put the editor in a vise. Reynolds leaned back in his chair and crossed his arms, a move that Nick read as a definite defensive position.

After a brief silence, Morton spoke again. "But is it worth it? This Suzie Alvarez—this wasn't her home. She was not part of our community. People like her are lawbreakers and should be locked up and deported, not glorified. Why are we making her out to be a saint?"

Nick and the C-Man did not react right away, neither wanting to antagonize the editor.

"You're right, Morton," Nick said finally. "Suzie was not born here and she was not a member of our community. But she lost her life while she was in our midst, and regardless of her immigration status, she was here and trying to make a living for her family, and now she is dead. I think our readers would like to know why and how. That's what makes this a story worth pursuing and what will ultimately make it a great story. We're not trying to make her a saint. We're trying to tell the story of how she died while she was among us."

This time it was the C-Man who nodded in agreement with Nick. "We are on to something big, much more than the death of one woman. I want to keep moving ahead, keep chasing it. With your support, I'd like to give the story at least another week to see where it goes."

A low moan rose from somewhere inside the editor. His visitors tried but could not discern its origin. They waited for him to actually speak.

For a few moments Reynolds merely blinked. "Well, okay," he said at last. "If you're both thinking this is the right way to go, I'll ride with you for a bit. But this had better be a really good story, and I want to see some copy by the end of the week. That's it."

He picked up his magazine. The C-Man and Nick jumped up from their chairs and headed for the door. As they moved into the hallway, the *Blade* editor could be heard chuckling again and then muttering to himself, "Why did the chicken cross the street? Ha-ha-ha-ha! Where do they get this stuff? Ha-ha-ha-ha! Great fun!"

As they rode the elevator back down to the newsroom, Nick thought it was a good time to drop a bomb on the C-Man. "Don't know if you saw it or not, but I left an expense account form and some receipts on your desk."

"Yup, I did, but I'm not covering your bar tab at O'Hare's. You're drinking too much again and trying to hang the tab on the *Blade*. Sorry, it's not going to work."

"Well, can you give me half of what I turned in? I can live with that."

"I'll take a look at it," the C-Man said. "And tell Balz I rejected his expense account form too. Five hundred bucks, most of it at O'Hare's. No way."

"Doesn't sound all that unreasonable to me," Nick said. "Dave does a great job for us. I think five hundred is realistic."

"Balz does not even work here anymore," Clapper said. "He retired and he works on contract. Tell him to turn his expenses in to Uncle Sam on his taxes—not the *Blade*."

The two men stepped off the elevator and stood in the entryway to the newsroom. Clapper changed the subject back to Morton Reynolds, telling Nick he was afraid the editor would shut the door on the Alvarez story if Nick couldn't pull it together fairly soon. He asked Nick how much more time was needed.

"I'm running on it as hard as I can," Nick said. But he asked for the assistance of Dave Balz.

Now it was Clapper's turn to be defensive. He wrapped his arms across his chest and shook his head no. "Why him? Why not Greta Norris or Gordon Smith or one of the others? Why does it have to be Balz?"

"'Cause you need the story in a hurry, and I need the help of someone I trust," Nick said. "I can work with Greta or Gordon, but I need Dave to push this piece into high gear. I will call him while I'm on the road today, and we'll meet tonight."

Clapper agreed reluctantly. "Okay, you can use Balz, but stay the hell out of O'Hare's. You guys have got a lot of work to do."

Chapter 18 — Tuesday afternoon

Monica powered her rental vehicle off Simpson Road in southern Huron County and onto an unmarked trail that ran adjacent to a cornfield for as far as the eye could see. She and Nick bounced along the unimproved road behind the four-wheel-drive pickup truck driven by Sister S.

The nun drove the truck in third gear, rolling and bouncing along the jagged path. Every time she hit a big hole that caused the truck to jerk and lurch, she looked in her rearview mirror to see if Monica and Nick were still with her.

Nick had suggested Monica drive during this visit to the Thumb because he did not want to torture his gold Firebird, which would not have been a good match for this obstacle course. The rental vehicle, a tan Chevy Cruze, could take the torment, they figured. Monica, driving slowly in low gear, held the steering wheel with both hands as the rocky road tried to rip it from her.

The two vehicles cleared a hill, and a large two-story barn, green with a light-tan roof, came into view. Behind it stood a ranch-style building that looked like it needed fresh paint and general maintenance to repair the holes in the roof. The leaves on two giant oaks rattled in the breeze coming over the hill. It was a pastoral farm scene that would make an appropriate setting for an artist to paint.

As they rolled along the path to the two buildings, Nick pulled out his cell phone and called Dave Balz. He had been trying to reach his friend since he and Monica left Bay City.

This time Dave answered the phone. "What's up?"

Nick did not have time to chat, so he got right to the point. "I talked with the C-Man this morning, and he's okay with you giving me a hand on this story."

"Did he authorize payment on my expense account?" Dave asked. "I'm broke. Gotta have it."

"Uh, yes, he did say something about both of our expense accounts," Nick said, glancing over at Monica. "I think we can win him over. But in the meantime, I need you to jump into this with both feet. We're getting pressure from the Worm to finish the story, and at this point I have no idea where it's going."

"What do you want me to do?" Dave said.

"Call Deputy Del and see if he's turned up anything since we met him. Has he gotten anywhere with the doc down in Muskegon who did the breast implants for Suzie? Anything new on the abandoned truck or who drove it? Has he turned up any new leads on the case? See what you can find out. We'll meet at O'Hare's tonight to see where we are in the story."

"I'll get right on it."

When Nick finished the call, Monica asked why they met at the bar all the time to talk about work.

"It's because they don't serve beer in the newsroom," he said. "Believe me, we have suggested it repeatedly, but the Castrator and the Worm won't budge. It's a pity, really. Think of the work we'd get done, how much fun we'd have, and the money we'd save."

Monica laughed. She said she was not much of a drinker but asked if she could attend the meeting that night with Dave. Before Nick could answer, a young dark-haired woman came out of the ranch building to greet the two vehicles. It was Maria, a friend of Suzie's, whom the nun had already briefed on her fate. Maria had recognized Sister S.'s four-wheel-drive truck and approached it first as the black half-ton vehicle rolled to a stop.

Sister S. and Maria could not appear more different. Maria, with dark eyes and long braided hair hanging loosely down her back, was dressed in worn blue jeans and an oversized red hooded sweatshirt. The nun's short, graying hair was tucked behind her scarf and cowl. Her billowing skirt whipped in the wind. She wore sensible flat shoes and a heavy knitted green sweater.

The two women spoke together in Spanish, and then Sister S. introduced the visitors. As they shook hands, Nick noticed two other women leave the ranch-style building and go into the barn. They kept their heads down as they walked, occasionally stealing side glances at the strangers.

Nick knew how excited Monica was to meet Maria because she and Suzie had been close. Sure enough, they talked to each other in Spanish so fast that even Sister S. could not keep up.

"JESUS, Mary, and Joseph," she said, loud enough to quiet the two women. The nun blessed herself twice and then kissed the crucifix that dangled from her neck. "Slow down, please, and English so Nick and I can fully understand what you're talking about."

Monica nodded, a big smile on her face. Maria invited her visitors into the ranch-style building, which was divided into three areas: general storage, sleeping cots, and a small kitchen with a one-stall bathroom. The building had been cobbled together from a hodgepodge of metal, wood, and plastic—very little insulation, but a cast-iron potbelly stove stood in the middle. Modest electrical service gave the sleeping area dim light. Nothing fancy, but it seemed clean and warm.

Nick noticed that most of the cots had handcuffs hanging from the front or back end. He asked Maria about them.

"It's punishment," she said, her gaze darting to the door. Talking about the cuffs and retribution made her jumpy, Nick thought. "If they think you're going to run, they tie you down with the cuffs. If you break the rules, sometimes they cuff you too. Juan and Janene hand out justice around here. She can be meaner than him, particularly with the women. Here is where Suzie slept."

The reporter perked up when Maria referred to Janene and Juan—finally he had met someone who knew them and dealt with them directly. He was excited to get Maria's full take on the notorious duo, but he also had to be careful not to rattle the young woman, who was obviously fearful when talking about them.

Monica and Nick approached the cot, which was under a window near a wooden support post. Sister S. had wandered off to inspect the bathroom, saying she hoped it was as clean as it had been in past visits. Monica sat on the cot and ran her hands over the blanket on top. She picked up the pillow and smelled it.

Nick examined the window and post. "How long was Suzie here?" he asked, noticing letters carved into the wood. He ran his fingers over the carving, trying to make out the words.

Maria said she had been assigned to the calf barns last winter. "She worked here through the spring until she was sold," the girl said.

"What do you mean, 'sold'?" Monica asked, her anger flaring enough to alert the nun, who was now inspecting the kitchen area. Monica's agitation brought her back to Suzie's cot. "Sold to whom for what?"

"I heard Juan telling one of the other women that Suzie was too much trouble—they were afraid she was going to get loose and go to the immigration department," Maria said, whispering. She sat down on a cot across from Monica while her visitors leaned in to hear her soft voice. "They whipped her and broke her fingers, but they couldn't break her spirit. So, Juan sold her debt to a broker on the west side of the state. We were told she was going to pick fruit and tend orchards, but that was the last we heard of her. She simply disappeared."

The nun looked at Nick and mouthed the word *goner*. Nick

nodded.

Maria's matter-of-fact description of the torture distressed her visitors too. Sister S. blessed herself and kissed her crucifix. Monica blew her nose with a handkerchief, unable to speak. Maria tried to comfort her, telling her how Suzie had become a big sister to her, offering her support and, most importantly, hope.

"She always believed tomorrow was going to be a better day," Maria said, patting Monica's hands, which were flipping the soggy cloth. "Suzie would tell me we were going to work our way off the dairy farms and into mainstream America. It would just take time, hard work, and a little luck."

Maria had worked the calf barn for more than a year, she said. She was eighteen and had come to work the Thumb dairy farms from a large chicken processing operation in Illinois that produced thousands of pounds of raw meat for grocery stores throughout the Midwest. When she was sold for debt with a dozen other women to Juan, it was generally viewed as a step up.

Maria told Nick and Monica she'd become impatient after Suzie left the farm. She'd tried running away herself, hoping to turn herself in to ICE, but was caught by Janene.

"I thought for sure I was going to catch holy hell," Maria said, quickly checking the nun's face after using the swear word out loud. Sister S. did not react; instead she quietly recited a Hail Mary while the young woman recounted a night of horror. "They hung me upside down in a toolshed one night and Janene was going to beat me, but the farmer—I think his name was Bud—stopped it. Instead, I was handcuffed to my cot, and they cut my food ration to water and tortillas once a day."

Monica asked why she and the others put up with such harsh treatment and the tough working and living conditions. "I don't understand why all of you don't run away at once. Turn these bastards in to the authorities."

Simple, Maria said. Everyone they saw on these farms had people—family back home in need of help, or family members who were working here or in other operations. "It's the only way we survive," she said. "We have work, we make a little money, and we give it to our people. It's not easy or pretty, but it's something. In Mexico, we had nothing. It's worse in Central America."

Nick piped in, "Sounds like what you put up with is the price of opportunity."

"Opportunity, yes. But also freedom," Maria said. "We dream of what you have and take for granted. We are willing to work long hours at jobs you won't take and in conditions you would not tolerate, with the idea that it will one day lead to good lives for our families. We are willing to make the sacrifices necessary. Isn't that the American dream?"

Nick scribbled her words in his notebook without comment. Nothing he could say or write could top her eloquence.

Sister S. suggested the visitors finish up at the property before they were discovered. Their visit was unofficial, and they had to move quickly or risk exposing Maria to more grief. She asked Maria to show them the calf barns so they would understand how the operation worked. Nick was eager to learn more—Monica, not so much.

Maria was proud to show off her work. She told Nick the women who worked with calves were almost their surrogate mothers. "We take the purebred heifers when they are just a few days old," she said. "We bring them here and start them in individual igloos at the south end of the barn. As they grow and get stronger, we move them off milk and onto regular feed. They go into big pens to be socialized, and after two years, they are ready to be bred or become milking cows. That's when they join the regular dairy herd. It's a continuous process. There are always calves here, sometimes more than a hundred at a time."

As they prepared to leave the bunkhouse, the reporter had one more question. He pointed to the carving in the support post near where Suzie had slept.

Maria and Monica bent down low to look at the letters carved into the wood: "*Más allá*," though the words that followed were scratched out. Maria said she had not noticed the words before and did not know what they meant.

"I can read the word *beyond*, but nothing after that," she said. "Any of the women who stayed in the barracks could have made the carving. Who knows?"

Nick asked Sister S. if the word *beyond* meant anything to her.

"JESUS, Mary, and Joseph, how in the hell would I know?" she declared, blessing herself twice and kissing her crucifix.

The comment drew laughter. Sister S. led the visitors out of the bunkhouse and toward the calf barn. Monica said the aroma was too strong for her; she would wait outside for Nick to take a fast tour.

A few minutes after Nick, Maria, and Sister S. had entered the barn, one of the women they had seen when they first arrived walked back out. She did not acknowledge Monica but passed by close enough for her to see that the woman's pinky fingers were crooked.

Monica could not resist. She approached the woman and spoke to her in Spanish, asking how her fingers were hurt. Had she been in a farm accident, or had someone harmed her?

The woman confronted Monica with her hands on her hips. Their conversation became animated and soon turned into shouting, which brought Maria back outside. She tried to separate the women, but they did not stop until Nick came over to check on the ruckus.

Finally Monica walked away, cursing the heavens. Maria and

Sister S. had heard enough to know the gist of the argument, but Nick asked for someone to translate.

"She told me to mind my own business and get off the property," Monica said. She explained she'd inquired about the injuries to the woman's hands. "She said our visit put them in line for retaliation from Janene and Juan. But what really got me pissed is that she said my sister had a big mouth and would still be alive if she'd been a good, hard worker. She's dead because she tried to stir things up—a troublemaker."

They watched the woman go back into the bunkhouse, slamming the door behind her. Maria tried to calm Monica by putting an arm around her. "That's Salina. Don't mind her. She's been here a long time and does not like change."

Nick was not comfortable with what he had witnessed. He feared the acrimony between Salina and Maria might come back to haunt Suzie's friend. He cautioned Maria to be careful.

"How much do you owe on your tab to Janene?" Nick asked, watching Monica out of the corner of his eye. "Do you have an idea when you will pay her off?"

"My tab is back up to three thousand dollars because I needed a root canal." She flashed a full toothy smile. "They took me to a dentist in Pigeon. Nice man, and gentle. Good with his hands. Don't remember his name, but I think it was Italian. With any luck I can be free from her in a year—if I don't have any more unexpected expenses."

Nick and Monica said they would stay in touch via Sister S. As they made their way back to their vehicles, the reporter asked what would become of Maria after she paid off her tab.

"Well, her English is good and she has some education, so I think she will be all right," the nun said. "Huron County has a mammoth underground economy. So many people work for cash here that adding one more to the pot won't raise an eyebrow."

Monica asked Sister S. if she would help Maria should the young woman run into trouble finding work or housing.

"Officially, no. I can't because she's here illegally," the nun said, kissing her crucifix. "But the Lord does work in mysterious ways, so unofficially I will keep an eye on her and give her a hand for Him if she needs it."

Chapter 19 — Tuesday evening

Dave Balz rolled into O'Hare's Bar & Grill with an extra kick in his step. He'd had a good day and was eager to share his new information with Nick, who had called on his way back from the Thumb. Nick said Monica would be joining them, and he had asked Tanya to stop by as well.

The reporter found an open table and caught the eye of Sassy Sally, the efficient and no-nonsense bartender who kept the notorious pub from getting out of hand by ruling it with a closed fist. Using sign language that only she understood, he motioned for her to bring a large pitcher of Labatt beer with three frosty mugs.

In no time, the pitcher and glasses arrived at Dave's table. He thanked Sally and asked if the Bay County sheriff had been in the bar since dinner. Dave needed to talk with the sheriff as soon as he could. In fact, he was so desperate to meet with him, he considered stopping by the sheriff's office near the county jail. But he dismissed the idea because catching the lawman in O'Hare's would be so much more fun.

As the two talked, Nick walked in the back door of O'Hare's and pulled up a chair at Dave's table. Sally poured him a glass of beer too and asked if he wanted a burger. Nick thanked her but declined.

After Sally had scooted away, Nick reached into his jacket breast pocket and pulled out the small blue ring box.

"Hey, before Monica gets here, I want to run something by you," he said. "What do you think?" He placed it on the table and pushed the box in front of Dave. Nick watched for a reaction but busied himself with his cell phone as if he didn't care what his best friend thought about one of the biggest decisions he might make in his life.

Dave stared at the box. Then he looked up at Nick and smiled as wide as his lips would stretch. "Nick, hey, buddy. We've been friends forever, and I think we always will be best buds. You didn't have to get me a ring. Really, it's not necessary."

"It's not for you, ding-dong," Nick said, trying to figure out the hurt in Dave's eyes. He opened the box, revealing a sparkling diamond ring. "It's for Tanya. I'm trying to build up the nerve to ask her—maybe even this week."

Dave grinned and gave his friend a soft punch in the shoulder. "I knew it was for Tanya, but I thought I'd jerk your chain a little first. How wonderful!" He picked up the ring and studied it for a moment, then replaced it and closed the box. "Why not ask her tonight? Go ahead, put her out of her misery. She'd love it."

Nick scooped up the box and put it back in his pocket. "I'm still testing out the idea, running it by people to judge their reaction. I've got to make sure I'm doing the right thing."

He also wanted to build up to the perfect moment and then catch her when she could not say no. Despite what Mrs. Babcock had said and the encouragement he'd just received from Dave, Nick was still unhinged at the prospect of popping the question. He was quite certain that Tanya would reject him while doubling over in laughter.

Within a few minutes, the front door of O'Hare's opened and Monica walked into the bar, hushing the watering hole. All eyes swung her way for a head-to-toe look at the dark-haired, dark-eyed stranger. She walked directly to the table where Nick and Dave sat, which sent waves of whispers washing across bar patrons like roiling surf.

Dave popped out of his seat to greet Monica. Nick motioned to a chair across the table from them. She pulled it out and sat down.

"Hi, Dave. Good to see you again," she said, smiling and taking off her light jacket.

Dave excused himself to use the men's room. That left Monica and Nick alone for a few moments. Nick took the little blue box out of his pocket again.

Monica's eyes lit up as she opened the box. "Oh, Nick," she said, holding the ring up to the light and turning it to watch it sparkle. "It's beautiful. Is this for Tanya?"

"Yes, it is. I wanted to see what you thought of the ring. I'm afraid it's not going to be good enough for her. That *I'm* not good enough for her."

Monica paused, then encouraged Nick to move ahead with the proposal. "I think it's gorgeous, and you're being too critical of yourself. Just pop the question and don't put it off. Is she joining us? Ask her tonight."

Dave returned to the table as Nick tucked the ring away in his pocket again. The older reporter poured Monica a glass of beer.

"*Gracias!*" she said.

"That means 'thank you' in Spanish," Nick told Dave.

Dave looked insulted. "I know what it means," he said. "In fact, I am quite fluent in Spanish."

That was a new one on Nick. He'd known Dave for ages and had never heard that his friend was fluent in anything but bar talk. Both he and Monica marveled at Dave with awe and respect.

Dave cleared his throat and eyed the upside-down Christmas tree hanging from the ceiling of the bar, as if it contained a magical language translator.

"*Si. Yo hablo Espanol muy bien,*" he said, pronouncing each word slowly and carefully. He checked the faces of his friends to see if they were still with him. "*Quiero muchos cerveza fria.*"

Surprised, Nick turned to Monica.

"He says he speaks Spanish very well, and he wants many cold beers," Monica said, disbelief crossing her face. "Very good, Dave. What else can you say?"

"That's it," he said. "Really, what else would a man need?"

Nick wadded up the napkin under his beer glass and tossed it at his old friend. "I don't think that qualifies you as a Spanish linguist."

The three laughed, and Dave suggested a toast. They hoisted their beer mugs and clinked them together. "To Suzie, may she rest in peace, and may her killer rot in hell," Monica said, sipping at her mug. Her face scrunched up as though she'd bitten into a lemon.

"I finally feel like we're getting somewhere," Monica said. "But I fear for Maria and Sister S. Taking us to one of the camps took guts. I hope it doesn't backfire on them."

Nick gave Dave a quick update on what he and Monica had discovered in the Thumb, then asked Dave what he'd learned from Deputy Del. His friend said he would be leaving first thing in the morning to meet the Emmet County lawman in Muskegon.

"I must say, Deputy Del surprised me." He sat back, guzzled the rest of his beer in three gulps, and eyed the half-full pitcher sitting between the threesome. "He's been working the case. He found out that the doctor who did Suzie's breast implants is no longer recognized by the State of Michigan as a physician. They took his license for a conducting a shitload of risky and dangerous cosmetic surgeries. We're going to look him up in the morning."

Nick poured Dave some more beer. "So, that means you'll be leaving bright and early, right?"

"Yup, this second glass does it for me," he said. "What about you, Monica?"

"Me too. I'm out of here." She took a second sip, which ended with the same sour expression on her face. She pushed her half-full glass to the center of the table. "I don't know how you guys drink this stuff anyway."

Tanya's entrance into the pub signaled Dave and Monica to disappear. They rose from the table, said hello to Tanya, and let her know they were leaving.

Dave grabbed Monica's glass and downed the contents in two gulps. "Waste not, want not," he said, a big smile spreading across his face.

Suddenly Nick and Tanya were alone together at the table. As they sat down, Nick took a deep breath and reached into his pocket for the small blue ring box. He placed it on the table and slid it in front of Tanya.

She looked at the box and said, "Is that what I think it is, and who is it for?"

"You, Tanya. It's for you."

She opened the box. Nick watched her face come alive as she studied the diamond. But she did not take the ring out of its holder. Instead, she closed the box and spoke to Nick in a low tone. "You can't just pass this off to me and call it good," she said. "If you want me to marry you, you have to ask me."

Nick was speechless—literally.

"I'll help you," she said. "Go ahead, we'll get through this."

Nick opened his mouth, but nothing came out. Tanya motioned for him to proceed.

He stood from the table and dropped down to one knee. Under the upside-down Christmas tree and in the shadow of his pants hanging from the ceiling, Nick steadied himself to pop the question. Other patrons at the pub noticed the familiar gesture and spread the word that Nick was about to propose. O'Hare's quieted, which might have been a first for the raucous watering hole. All attention turned to the couple as if something momentous was about to occur.

"W-w-w-w-w-w—"

"Will," Tanya said.

"Will," Nick repeated. "Y-y-y-y-y-y—"

"You," Tanya said.

"You," he repeated. "M-m-m-m-m—"

"Marry."

"M-m-m-m," he said, unable to force the word past his lips.

"Nick, focus. You can do it. Say, 'Marry.'"

"Marry," he repeated, gulping hard.

"Me?" she said.

"Me?" he repeated.

"YES!" Tanya shouted as O'Hare's erupted in cheers and applause. Tanya dove into Nick's arms before he could stand, sending the entwined couple toppling onto the floor. They kissed long and hard, rolling on the bar hardwood.

When they stood, Tanya declared for all to hear, "I love you, Nick Steele. I accept your proposal. We can elope and get married this weekend."

"Wait, what? Elope? This weekend? Huh? Hey, hold on, let's talk about this," Nick said, panicking.

But no one really heard him. Everyone in O'Hare's, including Tanya, was caught up in the euphoria of the moment. Strangers hugged each other and high-fived. Sassy Sally had her hands full taking drink orders, but she paused long enough to give Tanya a hug and Nick a kiss on the cheek.

"Congrats, you two," she said. "Really happy for you, but who is paying for all these drinks?"

Nick and Tanya wanted to be alone to enjoy each other completely and savor the moment. Holding hands, they slipped out the back door of O'Hare's, leaving the place in full revelry—the wildest Tuesday night party since New Year's Eve had fallen on the third day of the week.

Chapter 20 — Wednesday morning

Juan downshifted the Chevy diesel to make the turn onto Sopher Road, a two-lane gravel thoroughfare used primarily by farmers across the region. He was hauling a gravity grain wagon with a side-unloading bin. Shelled field corn trickled from the corner of the wagon. Farmer Bud's place was his destination.

After he straightened the rig out, he relaxed, his mind drifting back to the brief but ugly confrontation with Janene on Monday. He had not intended to hit her—he knew better. But discovering thirty-seven dead people in a truck had caused him to act poorly, or so he told himself.

At the same time, the incident accelerated Juan's doubts about Janene and her future in the business. She was getting older and had been hustling laborers in a high-stakes game of cat and mouse with ICE for years. Sure, she'd been busted once. But a short stretch in prison and a fifty-thousand-dollar fine were nothing compared to how lucrative her business had become over time. The redhead had been stashing away cash for years, a fact that had not escaped her partner.

Juan had seen the brochures and paperwork for Janene's Argentinian villa. He also knew where she hid the warranty deed to the property and where she'd buried her cash. If she were out of the way, he thought, he would have access to both. If Janene were to have an accident or simply disappear, who would miss her? Not the migrants she terrorized with her whip, or the farmers who quietly complained about being overcharged.

Juan smiled at that. He didn't need her anymore, and her growing caution and apprehension were slowing him down. He wanted piles of his own money, and the cars, jewelry, and women that followed

122

wealth. If he worked out a plan, he thought, he could get rid of Janene in a snap of his fingers should circumstances dictate it.

Juan checked his rearview mirrors and realized he was no longer alone: ICE agents tailed him in a four-wheel-drive pickup with an extended cab. His attention danced back and forth between the road ahead and the image in his mirrors.

Where in hell had they come from? he said out loud, as he continued down the road, waiting for flashing lights to start spinning. He could see the mailbox for his destination just ahead. Slow and steady, he thought; they had nothing on him and they would find nothing.

The ICE truck sped up, its flashers came on, and Juan pulled the truck and its trailing wagon over to the side of the road, watching his mirrors. Agent Stevens emerged from the driver's side of the truck. Another agent, weapon drawn, stepped out from the passenger's side. Juan jumped down from his cab too.

"Hold on there, stay right where you are," Stevens said, recognizing the diesel's driver. "Well, yippidity doo-dah—it's Juan. Now, how in the world do I get the pleasure of seeing you in these parts twice in one week?"

"Just lucky, I guess," Juan said, inching closer to the gravity wagon to watch the agents as they examined the cargo. He also noticed shadowy figures in the back seat of the ICE truck cab—two people. "To what do I owe the pleasure of you pulling me over? What can I help you with?"

Agent Stevens climbed the steel ladder attached to the side of the wagon and rolled back the tarp. He stuck his arm into the corn until it reached his armpit—nothing but yellow grain. He jumped down from the top rung of the ladder.

"Do you mind if I take a look inside your cab?" Agent Stevens asked, striding toward the running diesel truck. He pulled open the driver's-side door and peered inside the console between the two seats. Again, nothing out of the ordinary. A look into the back seat of the cab revealed a few empty beer cans on the floor.

Juan leaned against the side of his truck just a few feet away from the snooping agent. He wanted to appear casual about the impromptu inspection, so he lit a cigarette and inhaled deeply.

Then he froze, the cigarette dangling from his lips as smoke wafted upward into his eyes. A long, thin chunk of weld holding the corner seams of the wagon together had broken away, revealing red flannel cloth inside the wagon. Juan checked whether either agent was watching him. They were not.

He moved away from the corner of the wagon and engaged Agent Stevens. "Really, what are you looking for? Maybe I can help you find it."

Agent Stevens crawled on his back underneath the pickup in answer. The other agent, Harvey, did the same thing with the grain wagon. Next, Harvey pulled a five-gallon plastic bucket out of the ICE truck and placed it under the unloading chute of the gravity wagon. He cranked open the door to the chute a few inches. Shelled corn filled the container.

"You know what we're looking for," Agent Stevens said when he'd pulled himself out from under the truck. "You and Janene are moving illegals all across the Thumb. We know that. The only things we don't know are how and when. Only a matter of time before we catch you."

Juan edged away from the corner of the grain wagon and the exposed piece of flannel. He took a final drag on the cigarette, then pinched the hot coals until they fell to the ground. He stuck the butt of the smoke into his mouth, pushing it into his cheek with a flick of the tongue. It was loaded with nicotine and would make a good chew.

"Hey, I'm just a lowly farm worker," he said, closing the rear door of his pickup. He turned away from the agent and spat brown slurry at the ground. "I'm past due on getting this load of corn to the farm. Are you done here?"

Agent Stevens held up his hand to slow Juan down. "I just need to call this stop in, and then you can be on your way."

When Stevens had climbed into his truck, Juan made small talk with Agent Harvey, hoping to keep him distracted. They gabbed about the Tigers. Miguel Cabrera was in the midst of a hitting slump, and Juan told the agent he had the solution to the ballplayer's batting woes. "Miggy is carrying his hands too low at the plate. Too many popups and easy fly balls," he said. "When he is on, Miggy drives the ball to all fields." The agent nodded in agreement.

Agent Stevens opened his door and waved at the two men. "Okay, we're good here."

Juan wasted no time pulling away from the ICE agents when he was dismissed. He watched them get smaller in his rearview mirror. When they were four inches high and obviously not in pursuit of him, he took a deep breath and relaxed slightly, turning his attention to his destination: Bud's homestead. Juan hoped the farmer was occupied with other business. He didn't want Bud to see the wagon when it was unloaded.

Bud and his truck were nowhere in sight, so Juan drove the truck straight into the granary, where he opened the side bin door of the gravity wagon. More than six hundred bushels of corn drained out of the wagon and into shelled corn storage. Then Juan climbed the ladder on the side of the wagon and looked down into the box, which was empty except for the bodies of two men.

The bodies had been secured to either side of the box with rope. One of the men wore a red flannel shirt and the other a blue Detroit Lions sweatshirt. They had been shoveling grain in a silo when one of the support beams gave way, causing hundreds of tons of feed to collapse on them. Sad and tragic, but it was not uncommon for farm accidents to sometimes turn deadly.

Now, Juan had to get rid of the bodies. He walked outside and motioned to two men who were loading a hay feeder. They scurried to Juan's side.

"Get them out of there and wrap them in tarp," he ordered. "Then take them over to the toolshed and load them in the back of the refrigerated truck. Do it now. That truck has got to move today."

Juan hurried down to his office through the root cellar entrance to send a brief email: "Sending some logs your way today." He pulled a wad of cash, all fifties and hundreds, out of his pocket and stuck it in a wall safe, which opened with three twirls of the dial. Then he bounded back up the stairs to check on the bodies.

The laborers had worked quickly near the gravity wagon. The bodies, now rolled up in thick tarps, were already loaded in the truck, looking like bright blue logs. Juan checked on the work, then poked his head outside to make sure Farmer Bud was still out of sight.

He was. The truck rolled out of the granary and moved toward the toolshed, where men stood holding the doors open.

As Juan closed the door of the granary, he was hailed by Salina, who had hitched a ride to Bud's place from the farm where she worked. She told him Maria and Sister S. had brought strangers to the calf barns, though she did not know who the visitors were. "One of them asked about Suzie Alvarez. She looked like Suzie too. I thought you should know."

Juan shook his head and kicked at the dirt. He thought he'd swept out his worst problem. Now he had more troublemakers on his hands. But he thanked Salina and told her she had done the right thing. "Your good work will be rewarded on payday," he said. "Too bad some people only learn the hard way."

Salina nodded and walked away. Juan pulled out his cell phone and punched in a number. "Go get Maria and take her to the shed. I've got plans for her and the nun. We got another mess to clean up."

Chapter 21 — Wednesday morning

Agent Stevens said, "Well, that's Juan." He settled into his seat and picked up his radio transmitter but directed his conversation toward the back seat, where Nick and Monica had watched the whole stop. "I didn't expect to find anything today, but now you know what he looks like. Too bad Janene wasn't with him—you would've gotten a twofer."

Nick thanked the agent but wondered if they'd have a chance to talk with him down the line. "Same with Janene, if we can swing it."

"Well, we see them moving back and forth between these farms out here every day," Stevens said. "Sometimes they're hauling feed or supplies or waste. Very smooth—they know what they're doing." He cautioned Nick that meeting with either of them alone could be dangerous. "They're unpredictable. We hear plenty of crazy stories."

The threesome watched Juan make small talk with Agent Harvey near his truck. Through an open window, they could hear the two men talking about the Tigers and Miguel Cabrera.

Nick shook his head at the discussion. He had his own remedy for the Tigers slugger: "Miggy just needs some extra batting practice to get his stroke back. I wouldn't move his hands at all."

Agent Stevens opened the door on his truck and motioned for Harvey to come back, ending the stop of Juan and his corn wagon.

As Juan's truck pulled away, they continued talking about him, watching until he neared Farmer Bud's driveway in the distance. Nick asked the ICE agents if they knew where Janene's right-hand man came from originally.

128

Before they could answer, Monica piped in: his accent told her he came from Mexico, probably the barrio in Mexico City. "He sounds dirt poor," she said.

The look on Agent Stevens' face indicated Monica's assessment was good. Though Juan had invested considerable time into improving his English, he had still not knocked off the hard edges of his accent, he said. The agent's background check into Juan had revealed he grew up hustling to stay alive—pickpocket, small-bag pot pusher, con man, swindler, and petty thief.

Monica asked about the bond between Juan and Janene. Given his petty crime and street life background, she wondered what made them good partners and held them together.

"Rough sex is what we hear," Agent Stevens said, checking Monica's expression in his rearview mirror to see if his blunt response might have crossed a line. It had not, so he continued. "We hear from the people we've caught that Janene and Juan often get drunk and wild together. Their fights are loud and legendary, but so are the makeups."

Silence filled the cab except for the ongoing squawk from the radio. Agent Stevens started the truck, heading toward Bad Axe.

Something was bothering Nick. The story was becoming far more complex than he'd originally planned. If ICE agents had been tagging and investigating the couple for years, he didn't understand what was holding them back now. "If you've got informants and that kind of detail, why don't you bring human trafficking charges against Janene and Juan?"

"It's all bits and pieces," Agent Stevens said. He navigated the truck back onto the main highway and glanced back at his passengers in the rearview mirror. His face was hard, expressionless. "We have many of the pieces, but we don't know the full scope of their schemes. If it's a huge operation with tentacles reaching in every direction, I don't want to break off one tentacle—I want to bust the whole squid. So, we keep a close eye on them and pull them over whenever we can. Sooner or later, one of them will get greedy or hasty and make a mistake. Then we snag 'em."

Monica asked about Sister S., wondering if the agents were aware of her extensive knowledge of the labor camps and the migrants who lived and worked there. The question surprised Nick because he did not want to volunteer information about the nun that the agents might not have. Sister S. had been helpful to them and might prove to be even more useful as the hunt for Suzie's killer continued.

Agent Harvey replied, a warm smile easing across his face. "For years, she taught catechism at St. Felix, where mass is said in Latin and everything is very formal," he said, fidgeting in his seat. He clicked his radio off to tell the story from his youth. "She was a bundle of energy but did not have much patience for the kids who screwed around too much in class. She carried a long wooden ruler, and everybody dreaded hearing 'Hold out your hands.' The ruler hurt like hell."

Agent Stevens added that the nun was on their radar, but ICE left her alone. "We know she's plugged in to what's happening and keeps an eye on how workers are being treated. She speaks the language and offers religious relief. They confide in her, and she sometimes whispers to us off the record when she discovers bad things happening. Sister S. does way more good than harm. I like her."

Nick nodded, relieved they were gaining valuable information from the nun but also watching out for her.

The ICE agents drove Nick and Monica back to her rental car in the Walmart parking lot where they had met that morning. Before they spilled out of the ICE truck, Stevens reached into his center console and pulled out a flyer. He handed it to Nick, but Monica snatched it, her eyes widening as she read it.

Then it was Nick's turn to snatch it. He read it out loud:

WANTED
Captured or Cornered
Illegal immigrants

**They are flooding in, stealing our
jobs, and invading our homelands.
Fight for our rights!
Call ICE or sheriff's office
Be prepared to stand your ground**

Agent Stevens said he and Harvey had found a dozen of the flyers posted out in the country—at township halls, convenience stores, community bulletin boards.

"We've started seeing these pop up again," he said. "Vigilantes. We haven't heard of anyone being cornered or captured, but it's scary."

Nick asked if the agents knew who was behind the posters. He wondered if they carried torches, rode horseback at night, and wore flour sacks with eyeholes punched out.

Agent Harvey responded that they believed a small group of young men in the area hoped to whip up sentiment against undocumented people working on the dairy farms.

"We've seen it before," Agent Stevens said, scanning his passengers in the rearview mirror. "Local punks getting all lathered up. Trouble is, they won't take the dairy jobs—all they have to do is apply. The work's too dirty. It's beneath them. So, they run around, make a big fuss until the farmers get together and very quietly step on them."

Monica wanted to know if ICE had issued a public statement about the posters.

"We don't want to draw attention to the nut jobs," Agent Harvey said. "Don't want to make a bad situation worse."

Nick folded the flyer and put it with his notes for future use in his stories. He shook his head in bewilderment. "Obviously, there's an undercurrent of resentment about undocumented people working the dairy farms," he said. "I'm concerned about local folks confusing illegal immigrants with legal migrant workers who have been working on Michigan farms for decades. And what happens if someone gets hurt before the farmers put the locals in their place? Isn't 'stand your ground' code for 'shoot if you feel threatened'?"

"It's just bluster," Agent Stevens said. "They rise, they fall, they go away. Cowards hide behind anonymous posters. It's cheap talk. Didn't mean to get you riled up, but wanted you to be aware in case you happened to run across the flyers when you were out and about."

The two thanked the agents for the tour and information. Nick said he would be in touch.

As Monica drove toward Bay City that afternoon, she and Nick discussed what they had learned. Watching Juan interact with the ICE agents had been enlightening for both. Nick was surprised how well he had handled the brief detention. "Only time fear showed on his face was while he was smoking near the corn wagon. I noticed his eyes get big—rapid blinking—and then he turned and pinched the hot end of his smoke. One of the agents must have said something that hit his buttons."

Monica checked her rearview mirror and passed an old pickup truck on M-142 before they reached Elkton. She said she'd missed the change in Juan's facial expression; she had concentrated on watching the agents search the vehicle and wagon.

"I don't know, maybe it was wishful thinking, but I was sure the agents were going to find something worthwhile," she said setting the cruise control on her Cruze. "The whole search was so routine. I think they pulled him over for our benefit. Juan kind of stood there and watched. I don't know what to make of it."

The two drove silently for several minutes as they passed through wind farms on both sides of the road on their way through the agricultural communities of Elkton and Pigeon. Monica said she thought the spinning blades of the giant turbines, standing five hundred feet tall, looked as graceful as gymnasts doing cartwheels.

The reporter checked his phone for the time: late afternoon. He wondered how Dave and Deputy Del were doing in Muskegon. He hoped the two were continuing to get along, because any information they might glean from the Boob Doctor could be vital to their investigation.

The cell rang while Nick still cupped it in his hand—the newsroom calling. He answered it on the first ring.

Drayton Clapper's tough-sounding voice had a mellow tone, which baffled the reporter. The C-Man's manner on the phone was usually as subtle and quiet as a Mack truck rolling on the freeway. "Nick, thought you'd want to hear this right away. That nun you've been talking to out in the Thumb had an accident this afternoon. Brakes failed on her vehicle. She's hurt pretty bad—airlifted to Saginaw St. Mary's. Report just came over the wire."

The news hit Nick like a haymaker. He thanked Drayton and filled Monica in on what the C-Man had said.

The two did not speak for several minutes, letting the news settle in on them.

"Juan," Monica said without looking Nick's way. "It's gotta be

Juan."

That had been Nick's first reaction too. He wondered if Salina, who'd argued with Monica at the calf barns, had tipped off Juan that Sister S. had exposed part of their secret operation to strangers. "But would he really be that stupid and coldhearted to go after a nun?"

The question hung in the air. Neither answered. They didn't have to.

Chapter 22 — Wednesday afternoon

D ave drove around Old Town Muskegon looking for an answer to this question: Where can I find parking? After driving nearly three hours in a pickup, the reporter was ready to stretch out before embracing a cup of hot brew. He had hoped to find a spot somewhere near The Coffee Factory but was not having much luck.

As he turned the corner, Dave spotted Deputy Del standing outside his sheriff's department cruiser. The lawman peered into the window on the driver's side of the vehicle and adjusted his necktie. The Smoky-the-Bear-style cover was tilted cockily to the side.

Dave grinned. A tight space opened merely a block away, and he wedged his beater into the spot. A short walk would be good, he thought, to get his heartbeat up and some adrenaline flowing.

"Deputy, your timing is impeccable," Dave shouted when he reached the cruiser, where adjustments were still being made to Del's uniform. "Just got here myself, and here you are, looking good as usual."

Deputy Del smiled broadly and hitched up his gun belt before ambling toward Dave. He carried a large yellow envelope under his arm. "How's my favorite smartass reporter today?"

The two shook hands in the street. Dave thanked him for the meeting and gave the deputy a quick update on what Nick had discovered with Monica in the Thumb: Janene, the labor camps, and the two women who knew Suzie before she was sold.

"Sold? What do you mean, sold?" The deputy pushed open the door. A rush of warm air with distinctive aromas from the black brews hit them like greetings from old friends.

"Suzie accumulated some major debt with Janene," Dave told him. "She also became a problem—seen as a troublemaker. Her

135

debt was sold to someone on this side of the state, presumably to fruit growers."

After the two ordered java, Deputy Del revealed he'd picked up some interesting information about the Boob Doc, also known as Dwane M. Smithson, MD, and plastic surgeon.

Smithson had a big reputation as a doctor and businessman in the Muskegon area. The doc had grown up in Muskegon Heights, a bustling but poor nearby community. He'd attended Muskegon Community College and Western Michigan University and studied medicine at Wayne State University in Detroit.

The doc opened his first office in Old Town Muskegon in 1995, specializing in plastic surgery. He offered a full range of services for women, including breast augmentation, liposuction, nose reshaping, eyelid surgery, and tummy tucks.

But it was the experimental Botox injections that first got him in trouble. When women started complaining about treatments that left them scarred, disfigured, and suffering from various ailments, he came under intense scrutiny. Tests found foreign substances— fiberglass and wood filler putty—in his patients' bodies. Lawsuits piled up, insurance carriers abandoned him, his wife took the kids and left, and his debt became overwhelming.

That's when Doc Smithson started doing simple breast augmentations for cash on the side, Deputy Del said. Suzie Alvarez and many other young women became backdoor cash jobs.

Dave was impressed with the deputy's work. He asked if the lawman had talked with the doctor yet.

"Nope. With the blessing and help of the Muskegon County Sheriff's Office, I've been doing surveillance," Deputy Del said. He leaned in closer and lowered his voice, glancing around the shop. "His plastic surgery office is now closed, but he's got a string of businesses on the same street that cater to women—a deluxe salon, an accessory boutique, a chocolate and wine shop, and an upscale fashion outlet. I've been monitoring the alley behind the businesses. Women are still entering the plastic surgery office, but they're going through a building next door that shares a common wall."

Deputy Del opened the yellow envelope he'd carried into the coffee shop. Dozens of photographs spilled out onto the table, showing women entering and exiting the building next to the plastic surgery office. The officer said he'd taken statements from three of the women, who acknowledged getting discount breast augmentation from the doc for cash.

Dave sipped his coffee and pawed through the photos, thinking that some of the women did not look like they needed discounts. He asked what the deputy planned to do with the photos and statements.

"Leverage. I made an appointment for us to meet the doc," the deputy said. "Let's see what he's got to say about them. Supposed to meet him in fifteen minutes. You ready?"

Dave polished off the rest of his coffee and excused himself to the restroom, where he shot off a text message to Nick: "Deputy Del is on fire working the case. Going to interview Boob Doc, love it! Will keep you posted."

The sheriff's deputy, yellow envelope again tucked neatly under his arm, waited for Dave at the front door of the coffee joint, chewing a toothpick stuck in the corner of his mouth. Deputy Del had adjusted his cover. It was now planted squarely on his head, the brim pulled down to the edge of his eyes—Marine Corps drill instructor style. Dave thought the deputy's jaw seemed squarer, and his eyes had narrowed to slits. He looked ready to get down to some serious business.

The two men marched to the Boob Doctor's string of boutiques and shops. The lawman said he would take the lead when interviewing the doctor, but Dave was free to jump in to keep the questioning moving at a pace that would not give the subject a lot of time to think.

Dave reached into his jacket pocket and pulled out the Suzie Alvarez photo he had gotten from Nick. He showed it to the deputy, who nodded.

"I got a daughter that age," he said, glancing at Dave, who sensed a steely resolve that he'd not noticed earlier. "I couldn't quit thinking about that poor thing stretched out in the back of that truck—brutalized and then thrown away like she was a piece of trash. Just not right." Del plucked the toothpick from his mouth and tossed it toward a street trash bin. "Vowed right then and there to get to the bottom of it."

"We're really glad you jumped on this," Dave said, struggling to keep up with the long strides of the six-three deputy. "What you've shown me so far is impressive. Nick is going to love it."

A string of shops came into view, dark-brown, two-story brick buildings that looked vintage 1930s. But they stood sturdy and bright, alive with activity except for the closed plastic surgery office on the end. That was dark, with drawn shades covering the windows. The unlit sign atop the building declared its former name: "The Nip & Tuck Shop."

The deputy pointed at the coffee shop adjacent to it. "Doc says he has an office in the back, and that's where we're meeting him."

The shop was full of customers, some eating, others talking, most sipping java. Dave scanned the crowd, but the lighting was dim, giving the place more of a booze hall feel. A sign near the back indicated that restrooms and the office were straight ahead. He ordered two small dark roasts at the coffee bar while the deputy sauntered through the shop, the customers watching the lawman's movements.

Dave asked the clerk if the doctor was in his business office. The young man counted change back to Dave and suggested he follow him. The reporter waved for the deputy to join them, and they walked down a long, narrow hall past the restrooms. At the end, bright fluorescent light flooded from an open door.

The clerk stopped outside the doorway and told the men to make themselves comfortable in the office, which seemed to reflect the diverse business the doctor conducted. Posters and photos spotlighting women's fashion, food, wine, and the latest hairstyles covered three walls of the office. The fourth wall, behind his desk, contained dozens of photographs of women, shown nude from the bottom of the chin to the belly button. A sign above the photos declared "The Hit Parade—Making Mountains out of Molehills."

The men took seats in front of the doc's desk, surveying the room in silence. Dave's gaze settled on the photos behind the desk. The deputy leaned toward him and offered advice: "Try not to stare—it's beneath you. You act like you've never seen the female form before."

"I'll do my best. Still drinking it all in, and I'm feeling mighty thirsty," Dave said. "Doc must be proud of his work."

"I certainly am," Dr. Smithson said, standing in the doorway. He rolled into the office, welcomed the two men, and asked how he could help them.

Deputy Del identified himself and said he was looking into the background of a woman who was found dead in Emmet County. He explained that Dave was a news reporter assisting him in the investigation.

The doc asked if he needed an attorney present for the interview.

"It's up to you," Deputy Del said, nudging Dave to break his stare, which was boring through the doc to the photos behind him.

"This is very informal. We are just here to gather basic information—trying to find out what happened to the woman we found Up North. I'm not looking to build a case against you."

Dave pulled out his notebook and scribbled with blinding speed, occasionally slowing to sneak another peek at the wall.

The doctor, with his brow furrowed and his right index finger resting on his chin, nodded without speaking. He settled into his chair to study the two men in front of him. "Let's proceed, but I reserve the right to stop this interview if I'm not comfortable with where it's going," he said. "What do you want to know?"

"As I mentioned when we talked on the phone, the woman we found up in Emmet had breast implants with a serial number that came from your office," the lawman said. "But she had the procedure completed after your office closed. Can you help us understand how that could happen?"

"Well, must be some kind of clerical error, maybe a typo." A confident, reassuring smile spread across the doc's face. His gaze swiveled between the two men. "Don't know what else it could be."

Dave slid the photo of Suzie across the table. The doc studied the photo without speaking, but Dave thought he detected a hint of recognition on the man's face.

"Can you identify this woman? Did she receive augmentation from you?" Dave glanced at the deputy, who appeared ready to speak.

"What we want to know," Deputy Del said, pointing at the photo with his index finger, "is how she found her way to your office, especially if it was closed. Did she come to you alone? How did she pay for it?"

The doc did not respond. Dave thought he looked like he wanted to bolt from the room or jump through a window, except the office didn't have one.

"Gee, I don't know," the doc said. He gestured to the photos behind him. "I've helped many women over the years, so I don't recall this woman, though she is quite lovely and distinctive."

Deputy Del opened the yellow envelope and pulled out the photographs and written statements from the doc's patients. He spread them carefully on top of the desk.

"Doc, we know you've been operating your clinic while your license has been suspended," he said, pointing to the documents. "These women will verify that and say you took cash payments under the table. But we don't want to go there today. Please, take another look at the photo of Suzie. See if it jogs your memory."

The doc studied Suzie's photo again. "Hmm, maybe I did work with her. But she didn't come here alone. As I recall, she was brought here with two other young women, and the two guys with them, couple of young toughs—they did all the talking. They wanted three procedures on the spot and paid cash."

Dave asked what the women had to say about the operations.

"Not much. They were screwed up—in some kind of stupor," he said, shrugging as he leaned back in his chair. His memory had suddenly improved. "The guys wanted it fast, no messing around, so I did the jobs quick. Hey, I can put a set of boobs on a garage door if I can get the paint to peel back."

"Nice, real nice," Dave said, his temperature rising. "Isn't this a medical procedure? What if it was for your daughter or your sister or your mother? You're starting to piss me off, doc."

Deputy Del put his hand on Dave's forearm to cool him down. The lawman wanted more information and did not want to derail the interview too soon. He asked the doc if he knew where the men came from and where they were taking the women.

"The hotellos up in Traverse City," the doc said, eyeing the statements and photos spread out on the desk. Dave thought he was trying very hard to gain favor with them.

The doc produced a card that said "Free Pass – Admit One – Unlimited Access – The 19th Hole." "They said I could use it anytime. You're welcome to it, and if it helps you, great."

Both Dave and the deputy were delighted the doc had not used the free pass but indicated they were unfamiliar with the term *hotello*.

"It's a combination of hotel and bordello," the doc said. "Very exclusive, and access to anything your heart desires. Sex, drugs, alcohol, gambling—you name it. And lots of it." He laughed at the disbelief on their faces. "Are you two really Pollyannas?" he asked. "Come on," the doc said, leaning back in his chair to pontificate. "What do you think happens when all those men flood northwestern Michigan to golf, gamble, fish, and sail? They gotta have some playtime, and then they want a little more, that unforgettable experience. They got lots of cash and big appetites for the late-night, risky crowd."

The deputy asked what the doc knew about the men who'd brought Suzie to his clinic. Did he have a name or cell phone number he could share? Anything in writing—signed documents? To jog the doc's memory again, he tapped the pile of statements and photos displayed on the desk.

"No, it's cash—no questions asked," the doc said, fidgeting in his chair. "One of the guys was called Jake and the other Jesse. The card I showed you is all I got and all I know. I usually don't see the women again unless I get a bleeder. They can be a little messy."

Dave worked at hiding his disgust with the so-called doctor. He jerked his head toward Deputy Del and asked if he'd had enough. The deputy nodded, but Del wasn't quite done. He reached into the yellow envelope and removed one more photo. "Dave, let's see that photo of Suzie again."

Dave produced it, and the deputy put it on the doctor's desk side by side with a photo of Suzie stretched out in the back of the pickup truck, her bloodied head and neck in full view. The doc recoiled at the gruesome photo.

"Doc, I want you to look at these two photos good and hard," Deputy Del said, his eyes narrowed to slits again. "The scum you are helping with backdoor operations—they most likely bludgeoned this poor woman to death."

The doc held up his hands but looked away. "I'm a healer, not a killer. You can't put this on me."

"You're a quack, and a dangerous one." The lawman grabbed Dr. Smithson by the collar and pushed him down until his face was inches from the photos. "I want you to remember this for the rest of your life," Deputy Del said. "I want these pictures to haunt you until your miserable ass is planted in the ground. Then you'll be God's problem, and I have no doubt He will know how to handle the likes of you."

Dave was stunned by the deputy's reaction. He pulled Del's arm to urge him out of the office before something ugly and regrettable happened. "Come on, Del, time to go."

When they reached the door, the lawman turned and gave the doctor a final warning: "No more backdoor operations. My connection at the Muskegon County Sheriff's Office will have this envelope, and he will be watching your ass, waiting for a misstep."

The two left without offering thanks or saying goodbye.

Chapter 23 — Wednesday evening

Janene gathered her essentials on the bed and yanked a suitcase out of the closet. It was time to put together a getaway bag, she thought: passport and matching identification, a thousand dollars in twenties and fifties, a CD containing all her financial account numbers and passwords, a disposable cell phone, a change of clothes, a wig, hair coloring, fake eyeglasses, and extra sunglasses.

The task completed, she stretched out on the bed to relax and think about what she might have forgotten. Her plan was to drive to Port Huron, cross into Canada through Sarnia, and pick up a flight out of Toronto to Rosario, Argentina, the country's third-largest city. From there, it was a three-hour trip to her villa. Then she'd be home free and could live the life she had worked so hard for all these years.

Timing was the last detail for her exit. She needed a few days to figure out a plan for a final escape but knew that the clock was working against her. Her instincts told her the wheels were about to come off the rolling operation she had created. Janene's world had turned upside down when she and Juan discovered the thirty-seven dead laborers in the refrigerated truck. She could not get it off her mind. No sleep, constant headaches, lingering depression, and continuous sorrow and regret dogged her day and night. She had to get out, and get out now.

It was more than she had bargained for when she developed this business. People died for all kinds of reasons, and she and Juan had figured out a way to get rid of the bodies. But hauling thirty-seven bodies out of metro Detroit had crossed a line for Janene. If they had slipped up during the transport, she could have been sent to prison for the rest of her days. It was a close call that Janene did not intend to experience again.

Juan was out of control, she thought, and now he had become sloppy—careless and consumed by greed. He wanted piles of money, and he wanted it fast. The dead laborers weren't the only bodies piled up, either. Janene hated herself for having misread Juan so badly. She could not believe she had trusted him and become intimate with him.

A vehicle crunched up the pebble stone driveway of the old farmhouse that one of her contract farmers had allowed her to live in rent free. The sound was unmistakable. Janene jumped from the bed and peeked out the window.

It was Juan.

Janene pushed the essentials into her escape bag and tucked it under the bed. She was working on a fresh pot of coffee when Juan entered the house without knocking, which until now had been a definite no-no. He didn't say hello or ask how she was doing.

"We got a problem," Juan said, staring at the floor. "Actually, we got a couple of problems."

"No kidding," Janene said. "We've been having a lot of those lately. What is it this time?"

Juan said Maria had brought intruders to the property where the calf barn and barracks were hidden. One of the strangers was a news reporter and another was somehow connected to Suzie Alvarez. The third intruder was not a stranger, he said, but she was troublesome. "It's that damn nun—what do they call her?"

Word of the nun put Janene on high alert. Dread rushed through her body—and fear of what Juan or one of his men had done to her. "Sister S., and everybody loves her. She's never been a problem. In fact, the workers are much easier to handle when they're getting communion and having prayer sessions. Sister S. listens to them. She hears their suffering and comforts them."

"Oh yeah, well. What's the saying? Shit happens." Juan shrugged and looked down at his hands as if to check whether they were clean. "The nun had a little accident," he said, a smile crossing his face. "She won't be troublesome for quite some time—maybe never again, if our luck holds."

"You dirty bastard!" Janene leaped across the round kitchen table and knocked Juan to the floor, her balled-up fists flailing wildly at his head. She was angry with her partner for hurting the nun, but she also feared this "accident" would bring the force of the law to her door. "You are the most despicable man on earth!"

Juan swatted her hands down with a long sweep of his left arm. "Don't worry, I've got a solid alibi. I was nowhere near when it happened."

His words didn't satisfy Janene, who kicked at Juan on the floor, screaming, "If you had anything to do with harming that good woman …"

Juan laughed and pushed Janene away, slamming her body against a kitchen wall. She lay there a moment dazed and a little woozy from bouncing off the hard surface. He stood and adjusted his shirt, which had ridden up his torso while tussling on the floor.

"Maria was another problem, but she won't be anymore," he said. "I let the boys have some fun with her at the shed, and then she'll be shipped off to the western part of the state. They'll get their money out of her one way or another. As for Suzie's sister and the reporter, I've got some ideas on how to handle them too."

Juan turned to pour himself a cup of coffee, and Janene roared back into action. She jumped on his back, wrapped her legs around his waist, and pounded his head with both fists. This time he bent over frontward and flipped her back onto the floor, then smacked her in the face with a meaty palm. She went limp.

"Come on," he said, grabbing her by the hair and pulling her up off the floor with one hand. "After all that fightin' and fussin', we got some making up to do. Still got them handcuffs on the bedposts?"

Chapter 24 — Thursday afternoon

The intensive care unit at St. Mary's Hospital in Saginaw buzzed with activity. Nurses and orderlies drifted in and out of rooms so fast that a casual observer would think their movements were choreographed. Sister S. occupied the room on the right at the end of the hall, and Nick and Tanya could smell candles burning. They peeked around the corner of the doorframe.

Two nuns were kneeling with rosaries at the bedside of Sister S., who was rigged up with a breathing apparatus, three IVs, and enough wires and monitors to control a moon landing.

She had been airlifted to one of mid-Michigan's premier hospitals after her four-wheel-drive pickup suddenly veered to the right, dove into a ditch, and kissed a culvert near the edge of a driveway out in the farm country of the Thumb.

The result: Sister S. had two broken ribs, a collapsed lung, a broken arm, and worst of all, head injuries from hitting the steering wheel and dashboard of the careening truck. Doctors had induced a coma because of severe swelling on her brain.

In the corner of the dimly lit room stood a table draped in white linen. It held six lit holy candles (against hospital policy, but the nuns said the Lord would understand and forgive the violation), a tall wooden crucifix in the back, and three small statues—baby Jesus, Mary, and Joseph—in the front.

The nuns stopped their rhythmic recitation when Nick and Tanya stepped into the room and approached Sister S. Nick wanted to touch her hand but was afraid of disturbing her.

Sister Phyllis, known widely as Sister P., introduced herself to the couple. Nick said they'd heard about the accident and wanted to check on Sister S. They hoped they weren't intruding.

Sister P. shook her head no and smiled. "Ya know, they say people in comas can sometimes hear those talking to them or praying for them. I think she would like it if you held her hand."

Nick's paws swallowed her delicate right hand. He told the nun he was sorry about her accident and would pray for her recovery and relief from pain. Tanya bowed her head, blessed herself, and whispered a prayer. Tears trickled down her cheeks.

A nurse bounced into the room, barking out commands. "Okay, blow out those candles—you know the policy—and vacate. I need to get in here and check on Sister S. You don't need to watch."

No one questioned the nurse or her orders. The two nuns doused the candles and followed Nick and Tanya out of the room, but Sister P. hovered by the doorway, ready to dive back into prayer and meditation at a second's notice.

Nick asked her if the doctors had revealed a prognosis.

The nun winced, glancing back at the room they'd just left. "They won't be able to tell how severe the brain damage is until the swelling goes down," she said. "We might know something soon, but it could be days before they see results."

Nick and Tanya talked quietly about whether they should stay for a while or go back to Bay City. As they chatted, Nick heard someone call out a familiar name in the hospital hallway.

"Hey, Booger, what the hell are you doing way over here in Saginaw?" the man's voice said. "Huron County can't be safe and secure with you over here."

Nick's head swiveled in each direction, looking to see if Deputy Ratchett was anywhere in the vicinity. A little ways down the hall, the deputy was shaking hands with the man who had hailed him. The reporter moved in their direction.

"Deputy, how are you?" Nick asked, shaking his hand vigorously. "What brings you here? Do you know Sister S.?"

"Know her? Hell yes, I do," Ratchett said. "We grew up together—went to a one-room school in Huron County. She's the sweetest thing that ever was. We all called her Carin' Sharon. We were best friends until her folks shipped her off to the nunnery. First thing you know, she hatched out in the penguin duds and the rest is history, as they say."

Nick laughed. "Well, you're a little bit right. A convent is sometimes referred to as a nunnery, but nuns are not hatched like baby chicks. It's a long process to a spiritual life, and once there, nuns profess their final vows."

"Well, well, well, aren't you Mr. Smartypants," the deputy said. "All I know is that there was no more hanky-panky in the hayloft with her. No kissy face, no smooch-smoochy, no more Russian hands and Roman fingers. She became totally dedicated to the Church and helping people."

Nick gave Deputy Ratchett a quick update on the nun's status as they walked back to her room. By now the candles had been relit, and Tanya had joined the nuns on their knees, reciting the rosary.

The sight of Sister S. hooked up to machines was too much for the deputy to handle. He touched her arm and wept quietly. "Sharon, you're going to make it, honey. You can't go nowhere now—too many people love you and need you."

The deputy walked around the bed and knelt on the hard tile floor, joining hands with the nuns and Tanya. He bowed his head and tried to keep up with the prayers when he could remember the words.

The scene was overwhelming for Nick, who reached out and held Sister S.'s right hand again. He wished he could help her, and he was fearful the visit to the farm had led to her accident. The only noises in the room were the soft beeping of the machines and the murmured chanting of those engrossed in prayer. He could not remember ever being involved in such a tender, spiritual moment. It made him think a little harder about his future—and Tanya's.

On the way to Bad Axe, Nick had told Monica about his proposal to Tanya after Monica and Dave left the bar. Monica shrieked with joy when Nick revealed that Tanya dove into his arms, causing them both to roll on the floor of O'Hare's.

Nick gave her the full story, including the revelation that Tanya was ready to elope immediately. "It can't happen that fast," Nick said, glancing at Monica as she drove, hoping to reassure her he wouldn't postpone his work on Suzie's story. He shifted sideways in his seat. "I've got too much going right now. Plus, I would like us to take a little time to plan it, make it special."

But Monica's answer surprised him. "Sure you aren't pushing it off, hoping it won't actually happen?" she asked, staring straight ahead as they drove. "You've got to set a date and make it happen. Pretend like it's a deadline—that's something you know how to do."

Nick almost laughed at the memory now. But Monica was right, he thought, and Tanya would be happy with a set date. Making it a deadline would assure her of his sincerity.

Before long, the same hard-nosed nurse returned to the room. She did not mention the candles this time, and her commands had softened. Still, she wanted everyone out; the doctors were coming to check on Sister S. and then confer.

Deputy Ratchett grabbed a handful of tissues and blew his nose so hard it would have made Louis Armstrong proud. Others in the hallway stopped what they were doing to stare at the lawman.

"Hey, I can't help it. There's a good reason they call me Booger," he said, pausing to honk his horn again into the wet and weakened tissue. "Please, carry on."

Nick asked the deputy what he could reveal about the accident that nearly had claimed the life of Sister S. He had heard via the newsroom that the brakes on her truck had failed.

"Nope," Booger said. "Looks like the lug nuts on her right front wheel gave way—wheel came off and threw her into the ditch." The deputy looked back toward the hospital room as another nurse left. "Very suspicious. She's lucky to have slid along the bottom of that ditch instead of ramming a tree."

Nick revealed that when he and Monica first heard about the crash, their initial reaction was that Juan, Janene's right-hand man, had somehow been involved. The reporter said he was curious where Juan might have been just before Sister S. went off the road.

"Well, as a matter of fact, Juan was with me yesterday afternoon," the deputy said. "One of the farmers he works for had some property stolen, and Juan came into town to fill out the paperwork. He was there for hours."

Nick rolled his eyes, thinking that Juan was smart to have secured a squad room full of sheriff's deputies for his alibi. "Got to believe that's not coincidence," Nick said. The reporter asked Booger if he had any solid leads on what might have occurred before the accident.

Ratchett promised he and other deputies would give the accident full and thorough review. If anyone was playing with that truck before it crashed, he said, the truth would be revealed by hard-charging deputies who knew every mechanic in the Thumb. Boog said he owed it to Carin' Sharon to get to the bottom of what happened.

Nick asked if the deputy had heard from Monica, who hadn't answered her phone that morning. "I gave her your number so she had a connection if a problem arose during the trip."

"Nope." Booger fished out his cell and held it up for Nick to see.

Nick stepped aside to try her again. No answer. He left another message.

Chapter 25 — Thursday night

Dave pulled out a chair at his usual table at O'Hare's Bar & Grill. He was so excited about what he'd learned in Muskegon that he was almost giddy, and he hadn't had a sip of beer yet. He expected Nick and Tanya and Monica to come rolling through the door anytime.

Sassy Sally watched the reporter gather chairs around the table. She didn't wait for him to order—she drew a draft beer and took it to him.

"I take it you're expecting a few more to join you?" she asked, placing a napkin under the glass. "The whole press room this time or the usual crew?"

"Usuals, but I don't know when Nick will get here," Dave said. "He and Tanya are on their way from Saginaw. I think Monica will be joining us, and—who knows—we could have some others. It's been an eventful day."

The reporter took a long pull on his beer and licked his chops. He scanned the bar. Half full—lots of familiar faces. He waved to a few he would classify as friends, or at least as friendly.

One of the former was Michael Davidson, the assistant Bay County prosecutor, who was legendary for going after the town's corrupt businesspeople. But Davidson had also earned a reputation as a relentless defender of women. He was widely applauded for chasing human traffickers all over Michigan.

Dave and the prosecutor had known each other professionally for years. The reporter frequently used Davidson as a sounding board when he was assigned legal matters or court cases involving the lawyer's expertise. He was curious whether the attorney was familiar with the term hotello.

154

"Hey, Mickey, can I bother you for a few minutes?" he asked.

"Sure, Dave. I'll buy you a beer. How's that sound?"

"Like music to my ears," Dave said, leaving his half-full glass and his jacket at the table to hold it until his friends arrived. He joined the prosecutor at the long oak bar. They both fell under the distant gaze of Mona, the semi-nude woman in the large turn-of-the century painting behind the bar.

Sally brought Dave another cold draft as the reporter gave Davidson a quick overview of the story he and Nick were developing. "Ever heard of a hotello?" Dave asked. "You won't find it in the Chamber of Commerce directory or one of those spiffy marketing brochures they crank out for all things cherry up there."

The attorney took a hard pull on his drink and nodded. "Oh yeah. In fact, at least a half-dozen hotellos are in operation around Michigan," he said. "All you have to do is look where high concentrations of men congregate for fun—gambling, golfing, fishing, hunting, sports venues. They're designed for the high rollers who are willing to pay ungodly amounts of money to satisfy their urges while remaining anonymous.

"My experience is mostly in the metro Detroit area, but from what I've seen, they're all tied together," he said. "The common denominator is the women. Owners need a continuous supply, so they rotate the women between sites. Guys are always looking for strange and new. Once the women become common, they get shipped off to another state and another rotation, or they are disposed of."

"Disposed of?"

"Yeah, disposed, as in thrown away like a paper cup—wadded up and tossed in the trash," the attorney said, taking another gulp of bourbon and wincing like he'd swallowed broken glass. "Sorry, no part of human trafficking is pretty."

Dave nodded. He moved in closer to Davidson and revealed that their story involved human trafficking. "It's taken several wild turns," he said, scanning the bar to see who might be watching him confer with one of Bay County's top lawmen. "Every day, it feels like the story is getting bigger. We haven't figured it out yet. One aspect is a hotello up in Traverse City. May we call on you when we've gathered more information?"

Davidson nodded and said he would be happy to connect the reporters to an immigration specialist at the Federal Building in Detroit. They clinked glasses and polished off their drinks.

Dave turned away from the bar in time to see Nick enter the front door of O'Hare's. He was alone.

"Where's Tanya?" Dave asked. "Monica?"

"Tanya's on her way with Jennifer," Nick said, pouring beer from a pitcher Sally had just placed on the table. "As for Monica, good question. We haven't seen her all day, and we can't get her by cell. Maybe she misplaced her phone or somehow got separated from it."

Nick asked about the Muskegon meeting. Dave could barely contain himself. He raved about Deputy Del.

"You'd never have guessed it, but he's turned out to be a hard-nosed cop with good instincts," he said. "He's on this case all the way."

Dave described what he'd learned in Muskegon and from Mickey Davidson about hotellos. "Naturally, we've got to check it out," he said, a smile running from ear to ear. "Think the C-Man will question it on my expense report?"

Nick laughed and shook his head. "You don't get reimbursed, remember? You're not an employee."

Nick excused himself to go outside and take a call from the Garcias. When he returned, Dave could see the concern on his face.

"Monica is missing," Nick said. "The Garcias are convinced of it. They say she routinely calls to check in while traveling, but the family has not heard from her all day."

"Have they called the cops?" Dave asked.

"Even better than that," he said, taking a chair next to Dave to chug his beer. "They've called the Mexican Mafia. Someone is going to have hell to pay now. Big community meeting in the morning at Our Lady of Guadalupe. They're making Missing flyers and plan to organize search parties here and across the Thumb."

Nick's cell barked at him again. It was Deputy Ratchett. The reporter didn't say hello; he answered by asking if Monica had called the deputy. Dave could hear Booger say, "Hell no" before rattling on. Nick let the deputy know that search teams were being organized by a local church. The call ended with Nick asking for regular updates on Monica, and in return he would keep the deputy posted on Sister S.

"I just feel awful," Nick said as he tucked his cell in his jacket pocket. "Those two women were helping us, and now one of them is in the hospital and the other is missing."

"Well, I guess it sucks to be friends with us, huh?" Dave said.

As they talked, Tanya and Jennifer entered the back door of O'Hare's. Immediately Nick's disposition improved.

"You must have found a place to park your broom out back," Dave said to Jennifer, getting a jab in at his nemesis and trying to lighten the mood for his friend. "Did you leave your pointed hat and magic wand in the ladies' room?"

Jennifer placed her handbag on the table before responding. "I left them all outside, right across from your junk truck, the place where a sign says: 'This parking space reserved for assholes.'"

Nick held up his hands, asking the two for a temporary truce, but Tanya laughed. "Lord knows we can use a little tension relief," she said. "Seeing Sister S. stretched out like that, well, it just broke my heart."

Jennifer patted her friend's arm, telling her the nun would pull through and come back feistier than ever.

The others at the table nodded. They all wanted to believe she was right on the mark.

"That was very nice of you," Dave said, breaking the momentary silence. He leaned toward Jennifer. "If you continue the Ms. Roses & Sunshine routine, I may get to like you—maybe even give you a tumble or two in the sack."

Jennifer responded with a snort. "Maybe if you were the last man on earth. Wait a minute—no, not *even* if you were the last guy breathing. No way that's going to happen."

Nick and Tanya smiled and held hands underneath the table as their friends sparred and poked one another to the point that a passing observer might think they actually liked each other.

Chapter 26 — Friday morning

Nick walked through the back door of the *Bay City Blade*, expecting it to be just like any other day at the newspaper. He waved at press operators as they loaded the massive offset printing press with ink for the day's newspaper run. As he rounded the corner to head upstairs to the newsroom, the security guard stopped him.

"Nick, they're waiting for you up there," the security guard said. "Lotta grim faces. What did you and Dave pull this time?"

Andy's comments surprised him. Nick did not believe he was in trouble, but he paused and reflected for a moment just in case: Any recent wild escapades at O'Hare's? Nope. Any outrageous conduct in the Thumb? None that he could recall. Any hurt or offended news sources? Never. Any distraught readers who believed Nick or Dave had wronged them? None, at least in the last week or so.

Nick thanked Andy for the heads-up and bounded up the stairway, eager to find out what had caused such a commotion that it had ricocheted through the building and landed at the security guard's feet.

It didn't take long for him to find out. Drayton Clapper was waiting at Nick's desk when the reporter arrived. Without speaking, the managing editor motioned for Nick to follow him into the C-Man's office.

"Close the door," Clapper said, turning to face his employee. "I have to pull you off this story, Nick—at least for now. We received a threat against you early this morning. A note was found in the submission drop box overnight."

The managing editor read it aloud: "Tell Nick Steele that reporters who trespass in the Thumb get shot."

Perspiration leaked from the C-Man's forehead, and Nick could see that his boss was breathing hard. "We've called in the police. I talked with the editor and publisher this morning. This is serious, Nick, and we're not taking any chances. No story is worth your life."

"But Drayton—"

"No buts. You're off this story until further notice," the C-Man said, hands on hips and feet planted almost as far apart as they could go. "The cops have made a copy of the note, and they want to talk with you about the story you and Dave are developing. They also want to know who you've been talking to."

"I don't reveal my sources," Nick said.

The managing editor did not reply. He looked up just as Dave Balz rolled into the newsroom. The C-Man asked Nick to update his friend on what had happened because Clapper didn't have the patience to wage a verbal war with the salty, old-fart reporter.

Reporters had gathered in small groups across the newsroom, whispering among themselves. A few paused to point or stare at Nick and Dave. Word of the threat had rippled across their workstations and sparked rumors. Even staff members who did not think the newspaper should be developing stories about undocumented migrants were upset by the anonymous threat. They did not disperse until Clapper labored down their aisles, encouraging all to remain calm and return to work.

When he reached the far end of the newsroom, the C-Man almost ran into D. McGovern Givens, publisher of the *Blade*, who called the editor out into the hallway. Glass walls encased the newsroom on two sides. Nick—and most of the newsroom—watched the two executives talking for several minutes, both making their points with animated gestures. The conversation ended with big smiles from the pair.

They entered the newsroom together and approached Nick, who

was back at his desk sorting papers, pretending to be indifferent.

"Nick, you're back on the story," Clapper said, tilting his head toward the publisher. "Diane here would like to talk with you for a few minutes."

By now the whole newsroom had tuned into whatever was going on. The sight of the publisher walking side by side with the managing editor had caught most by surprise. They were hungry to hear the latest.

Givens stood directly in front of Nick, but her voice was loud enough for all to hear. She started by thanking Nick and Dave for working so hard to develop a story that was important to the community.

"Human trafficking is one of the great tragedies of our time, Nick," she said. "When I met with your supervisors this morning, we discussed the situation and concluded it was best for you to let this story sit until the police identified whoever made the threat against your life. However, upon further reflection, I've decided you must move ahead with your work. People are being abused and taken advantage of. Lives are at stake. We cannot stand idly by while suffering continues.

"When Drayton gave me the details of what you've discovered, I was horrified. This is modern-day slavery, and we must act. Keep working this story, Nick, and get to the bottom of it. But I want you to remain cautious. Let us know where you are, who you are meeting with, and what you are doing. I want updates hourly."

The publisher stepped back from Nick and nodded to Clapper, her arms folded. "Get him a bodyguard. I'll pay for it. Find a way to keep him safe while he continues. I also want you to get our whole newsroom involved. I need sidebar pieces on every aspect of the story—from the farmhands in the fields to the—what do you call them?—hodellos? Keep me posted."

The newsroom erupted in applause. Reporters, editors, photographers, and graphic artists whistled and cheered. Nick was delighted to hear that the publisher and the newspaper were committing fully to this reporting project.

Amid the outburst of emotion, Dave raised his hand, volunteering to visit the hotellos for business purposes only.

"The day I authorize you to go to a place like that will be a cold day in hell," Clapper said. "The deputy from Emmet County is going to the bawdy house in Traverse City. I talked to him this morning. You can interview him about what he discovered. I repeat, no reporters going into that place.

"But there is something you can do. Balz, you've now been officially designated Nick's bodyguard. Make sure he doesn't get hurt."

Dave thought about that for a moment. "I've been watching out for him for the last twenty years just for the fun of it, but now I'm going to get paid for it? I guess that's progress."

"Don't hold your breath waiting for the check to arrive. Just keep a close eye on him."

Nick checked his cell phone for the time, anxious to step away from the euphoria that had engulfed the newsroom. He told Clapper he was headed to the South End of Bay City to meet with the Garcia family. The C-Man asked Nick to check in with the news desk every hour, as Diane had said.

As the reporter left the *Blade* building through the pressroom, he gave a thumbs-up to Andy, who called out to him, "Go get 'em, Nick, and be careful out there. Let me know if you need me to watch your back."

Dave, trailing behind Nick, told Andy they'd be in touch if they needed some muscle.

The Firebird rested in its usual spot in the *Blade* parking lot, but this time when the reporter reached for the door handle, he hesitated. Could it be booby-trapped? Nick knelt beside the Firebird and looked underneath it. A small, square box about four inches high rested on the ground just inside the passenger's-side rear tire.

Nick jumped up, scanning the parking lot for suspicious movement or activity. He checked across the street and down the block, wondering if he should call the cops to alert the bomb squad.

Bennie, the Adams Street drifter, shuffled down the sidewalk toward him. "Hiya, Nick," Bennie said, pausing to pick up a discarded cigarette butt. He held it at eye level, straightened out the end that had been snuffed out, and stuck it between his lips. "You got a light?"

Nick shook his head, thinking he should tell Bennie to stand clear or move to the other side of the street.

But Bennie had spotted the little box beside Nick's tire. Before the reporter could stop him, the man had picked up the box and glanced inside. Empty. He tossed it in the gutter.

Nick and Dave laughed, the tension of the moment eased.

Paranoia, Nick thought, had become his companion. "Screw it—living in fear is not really living," he told his partner and newly anointed bodyguard. He jumped into the Firebird and turned the ignition without hesitation. The massive V-8 rumbled to life.

As Dave waited for his friend to unlock the passenger's-side door, Nick pulled away from his parking spot, leaving Dave waving his arms and jumping up and down. "Wait a minute!" Dave shouted. "I'm your bodyguard. Come on. I look like Kevin Costner—all the ladies say so. I can't protect you while I'm standing here."

Dave ran for his pickup but realized his keys were still in the newsroom. He'd have to catch up to Nick.

* * *

Nick traveled south on Washington Avenue, still shaking his head in disbelief. The last time the reporter had been threatened, a union boss had vowed to cut off his testicles and feed them to dogs because of an article Nick wrote suggesting bribes and kickbacks had been part of contract negotiations. Ouch!

That threat did not amount to anything more than hot air, and Nick had filed it away with a handful of other empty warnings he'd received over the years.

But this story was different from any others he had developed. Suzie was dead, Sister S. was in the hospital surrounded by chanting nuns, Monica appeared to be missing, and Nick had been threatened with bodily harm.

Frankly, the events that were unfolding scared him. He worried about endangering others who were close to him—should he suggest that Tanya stay in Ann Arbor until he was finished with the story? He wondered if it was safe for her to be around him at all, or whether the lowlife animals who had threatened him might target Tanya to chase Nick off the story.

He figured that could drive her crazy—one day he proposes marriage to her, then a few days later he gets a death threat and asks her to blow town. Nick tried calling Tanya, but she did not pick up. He left a message, hoping to conceal his fear and project an aura of calm: "Hi, Tanya, wanted to let you know we received a threat at the newsroom. It was directed at me. Probably not anything, but I wanted you to be aware. Keep your eyes open, don't take chances, watch out for strangers. Catch you later. Love you."

What about his apartment building and Mrs. Babcock? Nick thought next. He was glad she had Jenni. Nick jabbed at his cell phone with his thumb, but she did not answer either. He left a message suggesting she stay alert—and keep Jenni close.

In the distance Nick could see a crowd of women dispersing in front of the Garcia home, carrying Missing flyers. Most had children attached to outstretched hands.

He pulled into the driveway. Inez and Carlos Garcia stood on their front porch, shouting encouragement in Spanish to those walking away. Inez waved at Nick, inviting him into the Garcia home. He had already decided not to tell them about the note left at the *Blade* because he knew they would worry about it, and they were already concerned for Monica.

"Hola, Nick," Inez said, leaning over the porch rail. "You just missed it. We're getting the word out across the Latino community."

The reporter shook hands with Carlos, and the three sat in rocking chairs on the porch. The floor was covered with wood shavings. To burn off nervous energy, Inez said, Carlos whittled toy animals for neighborhood children.

The Garcias hoped Nick had an update from Monica. They also asked after Sister S. Nick had mentioned the nun's vehicle crash when he spoke to them earlier.

"I wish I had good news to share, but I simply do not," Nick said, leaning back in his chair, which squeaked as the rails of the rocker rubbed the shavings. "Sister S. is about the same, but I'm expecting another update from the nuns at the hospital. Nothing new on Monica. I was hoping you'd heard from her."

Carlos remained silent with his head down, his thick fingers working the blade against the wood. Remaining silent was not something Inez was good at or accustomed to. She asked Nick how much danger Monica faced, saying they had become attached to the young woman in the short time she had stayed with them.

"Don't know. The longer she goes missing, the harder it usually is to pick up the trail," Nick said, gazing down at the chips piling up on the deck. "We got on this pretty fast, though, so I am hopeful."

He asked Inez if she had checked Monica's room since the woman went missing.

"I took a quick peek to make sure she hadn't slipped past us and was in there sleeping," Inez said. "But I didn't look through her things. I didn't want to invade her privacy."

Nick nodded, saying that he understood, but taking a look might give them a lead as to what she was planning to do or where she might have gone.

Carlos, quiet and pensive, stopped whittling and put down his knife and wood. "Follow me," he said, leading Inez and Nick into the house and up the stairway to the room Monica used. He wanted to be involved and help if needed. He turned the doorknob and pushed the door open, then stepped back for his wife and the reporter to peer inside.

Neat and tidy was Nick's first impression. The double bed's coverlet was drawn so taut, it did not look like the bed had been slept in. A desk with a Bible sat in the furthest corner. Multicolored sticky notes were lined up along the edge of the desk. A jacket hung from the back of the chair, and on top of the tall, dark wood dresser was a rectangular box. A small suitcase and duffel bag lay at the bottom of the closet.

"Do you mind if I poke around a little?" Nick asked Inez, who did not object. Carlos had already retreated downstairs to his rocker on the porch.

Nick started with the jacket, which had two side pockets. One held salt packets from McDonald's; the other was empty. But an inside pocket yielded a slip of paper with a phone number. Inez perked up. Would the note help locate Monica? she asked.

"Don't know yet," Nick said, "but I'll check it out. Could be anything." He stuck the note in his front pants pocket.

Next he leafed through the Bible in case it contained any loose notes. It did not. The sticky notes were pretty colors, but none had useful information for the reporter either.

The dresser drawers contained clothing and a folder with information about funerals and transporting bodies to foreign countries. Nick asked Inez to sort through the clothing in the drawers because he didn't feel comfortable looking at Monica's personal items. Inez, however, did not find anything of value.

Meanwhile Nick had checked the head of the bed and noticed clothing in a pile on the floor—bloodstained clothing. Nearby was the evidence box that had held Suzie's clothes. Nick moved toward the pile, but Inez objected, stepping toward the reporter. She told him she didn't like the idea of handling the clothing of a dead person. .

"I don't feel right about this," she said, placing her hands on either side of her face. "I didn't know Suzie, but this feels unholy to me."

Nick asked Inez if anyone but Monica had been in the room. She shook her head no—which told Nick that Monica must have been examining the clothing and had left in a hurry. It was the only thing in the room out of place.

He lifted the blouse first—light-blue denim with white buttons down the front. The collar, soaked in dried blood, was torn on one side. No pockets on the front. The image of a bald eagle adorned the back, the bird's head obscured by blood. The shirttail was torn and muddy.

Under the shirt lay a pair of canvas navy-blue work slacks. Nick lifted the pants, which were spotted with dried blood in large circles down the legs of the garment. Copper-colored rivets attached the pockets to the canvas, front and back. And one of the front pockets held a slip of paper with another phone number. Nick studied the number and grimaced. He would call both numbers later.

The reporter was folding the slacks when he noticed hand stitching on the inside waistband of the garment. He looked closer. The Spanish words on one side seemed familiar; the other side of the waistband contained hand stitching as well, but it had been torn, perhaps when Suzie's body was dragged. He showed the words to Inez, who had watched the search intensely. She leaned forward for a closer look but did not get near enough to touch it.

"It says, 'Beyond the bridge,'" she reported, then examined the side that was torn. "First part says, 'you will find,' and I can't make out the rest." She drew back, asking why Nick thought the stitching was in a place where no one would see it.

"I think you just answered your own question," he said. "She didn't want her captors to see it."

"What do you suppose it means?"

The reporter wrote the translation in his notebook, then laid the slacks on the bed so he could take photos of the words with his cell. "No idea," he said. "But we saw some of the same words etched into a post near Suzie's cot at the calf barns in the Thumb. Suzie went to quite a bit of effort to leave these notes, so they gotta mean something."

Nick felt inside the pockets of the work pants. They were empty, but a small watch pocket in the front, under the waistband and below a belt loop, had a safety pin in it. The reporter tried to pull out the pin with his index finger, but it was attached to the inside of the pocket—and secured some kind of paper. He pulled the pocket inside out. The pin held a dollar bill, folded up to the size of a book of matches.

"What did you find?" Inez asked, intrigued. She no longer seemed put off by the sight of dried blood.

Nick had unfastened the dollar bill and was examining both sides. "Interesting," he said, holding the bill up to the light. Some of the letters and numbers on the bill had been circled, and though they didn't appear to spell out anything, it was enough for Nick. He figured Monica had not found the dollar bill, because it was still folded and pinned inside the pocket.

The messy clothes pile and the stitching told Nick that Monica might have gone to the calf barns and left in a hurry. He figured she would have wanted to check the post in the barracks where Suzie had etched similar words.

Nick told Inez what he'd discovered but did not mention the calf barns or Monica's confrontation with Salina. But Nick could not help but believe Monica's disappearance and Sister S.'s crash were somehow connected to that visit.

As Nick told Inez he was heading back to the Thumb, he was interrupted by the clunking and banging of Dave's beater truck as it rolled up in front of the Garcias'.

"Hey, buddy," Dave called out when Nick appeared on the porch. "I'm supposed to protect you. Keep my eyes sharp so you don't get hurt. I can't do that if you run away from me."

"Sorry," Nick said. "Thought you were right behind me." Both reporters knew that was fiction. Nick was not used to moving with a shadow, and he did not want to be slowed down. "I'm heading back to the newsroom to start putting my notes together," he said to Dave. "I plan to stick around town tonight, then go back to the Thumb tomorrow. I'll keep you posted so you know where I am."

Dave thanked him. He asked if anyone had been watching the Firebird while Nick was inside the house.

Carlos raised his hand with the carving knife still in it. "I've been sitting on the porch since we took him up to Monica's room. Nobody messed with it, though I checked it out pretty good. Sweet ride."

Chapter 27 — Friday morning

*P*lunk, *plunk, plunk*—the sound of water drops plopping into a bucket. Monica blinked repeatedly to push away the darkness. It would not go. The room where she was stretched out on the cold, hard floor was as dark as a cave. She sat up but still could see nothing, not even the hand in front of her face. For a moment she thought she'd gone blind.

Her head ached, a slow, rhythmic pounding in sync with the pounding in her chest. Her fingers found a knot the size of a golf ball on her noggin. As she gingerly rubbed the bump, she felt the edges of a small cut, and what she guessed was dried blood flaked and fell onto her collar, then to her neck. She wondered how long she'd been unconscious.

The last memory Monica had before waking up in this hellhole was finding Maria at the calf barns in the Thumb. She'd discovered the farm worker unresponsive and naked under a blanket in her bunkhouse bed. When she pulled back the cover, Monica could see a dozen burn marks in very sensitive areas of Maria's body. She tried to rouse Suzie's friend, but a blow to the back of her head put the lights out.

Now, all she could hear were the dripping water and her own rapid breathing. Monica felt the floor with her fingertips, sweeping across the hard surface in a full circle around her. The floor was gritty and grimy. She felt the sharp edges of small stones. No taste or smell to the air, other than a damp mustiness. She crawled toward the sound of the dripping water, which took her to two buckets in one corner of the room—one half filled with water and the other empty. She stood carefully, but she could not detect the origin of the dripping.

170

Monica wanted to call out for help but decided against it until she could get her bearings. Using her hands again, she felt along the wall, slowly making her way around the four-corner room. The walls were made of stone, sharp edged, with some kind of cement mortar. Her fingers ached.

Finally she found a wooden door, though she could not locate any kind of handle or lock—no window or peephole either. She tried smelling along the edge of the door, opposite the hinges. More damp and cold. In fact, she could not detect anything but the must.

"Hello, can anybody hear me?" she shouted at last. No response. She waited a moment, then repeated the question, this time louder and with more authority. Again, nothing.

Monica took another tour of the room, counting the paces between corners, using her size 6 shoes—heel to toe—to measure the space. It was about fifteen by fifteen feet.

Now it was time to scream. "Hey, can anybody help?"

There was no response. Monica returned to the door, thinking her voice might have a better chance of penetrating wood. She was about to shout again, when she thought she heard footsteps echoing beyond the door.

Sure enough, a few moments later the door moved. A clanging sound told her the lock was opening. Then the door swung open. Dim light flooded the room, half blinding her.

"You can scream your guts out, but it won't do you no good," came a man's voice, deep and raspy, like a smoker's. A tall, thick, shadowy figure stood in the doorway, but Monica could not see much else. She listened intently, hoping to hear something beyond his words. "We can do things easy, or we can do things the hard way. Your call. You may not like the easy way, but I guarantee you're not going to like the hard way."

Monica demanded to know where she was and why she was

being held captive. The shadowy figure laughed, the rasp giving way to a hacking cough.

"Shut yer yap," he said, delivering a numbing backhand to the side of her head, where the result would be hidden by her hair. "I'm in control here, and you're going to do exactly what you're told, or I will beat you into the next county. Got it?"

The blow knocked Monica to the floor, her head spinning. She felt nauseous and for a second she thought she might pass out.

The man pointed to the buckets in the corner of the room. "The one with water in it is for drinking. The other one is for pissing. Don't make a mess or you will be cleaning it up with your tongue. Got it?"

"Food. I need food. I'm hungry," Monica said, rising to her knees and trying to bring the shadowy figure into focus. She still could not see his face clearly.

"You will eat when I bring you food," he said. "I'm going to starve you for a while to get the last bit of fat off your body and teach you obedience. You get a handful of food for good behavior. Bad behavior will only get you hungry and knocked around. I was nice to you today. Next time I have to deliver discipline, you won't forget it. Got it?"

Monica did not respond. She tried to stand just as the shadowy figure backed out of the room and slammed the door shut, returning the cell to total darkness. The lock clanked into place.

As she pulled at the door's edge with her fingertips, she heard the faint, distant sound of metal banging in the distance. Then came the shadowy figure's muffled commands and a weak, soft response from a female voice. She wondered how many others were being held—and why.

Monica held her breath, hoping to hear more clearly, but it was futile. Another rattle of steel told her the man had finished. She listened for further sounds of footsteps or doors opening but heard nothing save the *drip, drip, drip*.

Monica shouted into the cracks between the planks of the door, "Hello, can you hear me?"

No response, but she was sure someone was there. "I heard you!" she screamed into the door. "I know you are trapped here too."

Frustration rushed through her. She beat the door with both fists, but it did not rattle or give. A hard kick only resulted in sore toes.

Finally she yelled as loud as she could, "Maria, is that you? Can you hear me? HELP!" More silence.

Monica returned to the wall across from the doorway and sat on the floor, pulling her knees up under her chin. She closed her eyes and prayed.

No one she cared about knew where she was, and she didn't know how they could find her. Here she was, locked in a dungeon in a strange country with nothing but the clothes on her back. Her cell phone and purse, with identification and passport, were gone. She was alone, cold, and afraid.

Now what?

Chapter 28 — Friday afternoon

At two thirty Nick walked into Murphy's Bakery on M-53 in downtown Bad Axe. He was scheduled to meet Deputy Ratchett and Agent Stevens from ICE. Both officers were late.

The reporter ordered a large pot of coffee and a half-dozen glazed donuts. When the waitress brought the order to his table, she asked if he was new in town. Her nametag identified her as Trixie. She was tall and slender, a couple of years out of high school, and her hair and eyes were as dark as a moonless night. Her apron sported big polka dots.

"Yes, I am," Nick said.

Trixie poured hot, steamy brew into Nick's mug. Her gaze darted between the filling mug and Nick's eyes.

He unfolded the large paper napkin and placed it on his lap. "Why do you ask? Do I look that out of place here?"

"Kinda. Only guys who wear suit jackets in here are lawyers, and I been to the courthouse enough over the last few years to know every one of them. Ain't seen you before."

Nick introduced himself and shook Trixie's hand. He explained that he was working on a story about undocumented workers in the Thumb.

"Illegals? Lots of them working on farms up here," she said. Trixie glanced over her shoulder to locate her supervisor, who stood at the cash register at the end of the front counter, a position where he could watch all the tables in the place. He did not like the employees getting too friendly with customers. "They're just trying to build a life, trying to figure out how to get ahead."

"You seem to know quite a bit about undocumented workers," Nick said. He was keeping an eye on the manager too.

174

"Know enough," she said, moving to the next table with her coffee pot.

Booger and the ICE man entered the bakery, and Trixie returned to fill their mugs. Nick thought she seemed nervous, but he couldn't tell if it was caused by the presence of the cops or the eagle eyes of the supervisor. She told the men she would check back on them.

Before the trio could tear into the coffee and donuts, Nick asked the lawmen if they had new information to share.

"Now, wait just a gol-durned minute," Booger said, reaching for the sweet goo. "I'm hungry. I'm a multitasker—I can eat, drink coffee, and talk at the same time."

Agent Stevens agreed, reaching for his share. Nick thought it better to let them feed. He settled in and watched Trixie dance between tables with full coffee pots in each hand, asking, "Regular or decaf?" in a soft, sing-song voice.

While the men grunted, moaned, and slurped, Nick dug into his jacket pocket for the slip of paper where he'd transcribed the circled letters and numbers from the dollar bill found in Suzie Alvarez's pocket. He pushed the slip of paper between the two men. It read "TEPDENMCL11612." They both studied it as they chewed.

"I was hoping you could tell me what it means," Nick said, explaining when, where, and how he'd found the dollar bill. "Take it with you—maybe it will make sense to you later."

Booger's face scrunched up in pain as he copied down the numbers and letters into his cell phone, which had been overloaded with selfies. "Damn, Nick, this is like one of them brain teasers. Numbers and letters were never my strong suit. I'll get my sister to take a look—she graduated at the top of her class."

The ICE man folded the slip of paper and put it in his pocket. "At first I thought it might be a license plate, but there's way too many numbers and letters. Will pass it around, see if it clicks with anybody."

Nick asked if either man could tell him what they had learned about the accident Sister S. had had, or if they'd picked up any tips that might lead them to Monica's whereabouts. He noted the nun's condition was stable.

"We're working it," Booger said, explaining that the investigation was in full swing. "Mechanics are pretty convinced the nun's wheel was tampered with, but we have no witnesses to the accident, and Sister S. is not communicating with anyone but the Almighty right now. We'll get a tip or a break in it, hopefully soon."

Agent Stevens seemed less optimistic about finding Monica. She'd last been seen filling up for gas at a convenience store in Sebewaing on the day she went missing, he said. "Her rental car turned up at Metro Airport in Detroit. Are you sure she didn't give up and fly home?"

"I can't see that happening," Nick said, pushing his coffee cup to the center of the table. The caffeine made him jumpy, and he was already on edge. "She was totally devoted to finding out what happened to her sister, so I don't think she would just pull up and leave. She didn't even grab her personal things from the Garcias' or say goodbye."

Deputy Ratchett suggested the search parties and flyers might bring better results. "I know it's tough, but you've got to be patient," he said, licking his fingers while polishing off the last donut. "Lots of people working this. We'll turn up some leads."

The lawmen finished their coffee and sweets. Agent Stevens got up from the table to leave first. Nick wondered if he had any new information on the vigilantes. He was a little concerned about the folks from Bay City who'd fanned out across the Thumb, circulating flyers to find Monica. He hoped they would not cross paths with the people bent on cornering or capturing undocumented immigrants, which might prompt conflict—or worse.

"Nope—probably crawled back under their rocks," Stevens said. "Booger is all over this too. He knows the local riffraff better than I do."

When the agent had cleared the door to the coffee shop, Nick asked Deputy Ratchett a question he hadn't wanted Stevens to hear. "I'm looking for another angle to help round out this reporting project and give it more depth and context. Do you know anyone who came here as an illegal immigrant but then became a citizen?"

Deputy Ratchett thought about the question while he licked his fingers again and swept crumbs off the table. He checked his watch. "Go down to the courthouse and look for a guy cutting grass. His name is Ronaldo. This time of day, he should be just about finished. Tell him I sent you. He's got a hell of a story."

The reporter made a note in his cell phone and thanked Booger. Deputy Ratchett headed for the door but grabbed a donut off Trixie's tray and thanked her on his way out.

When Trixie checked on Nick, he asked if she happened to know the landscaper Ronaldo.

"Sure do. He's my dad," she said, pausing alongside his table. She glanced out the front window at the officers walking away from the café. "Why do you ask? Is he in some kind of trouble? He's a good man who lives a clean life."

Nick grinned and shook his head no. He reported what he'd learned from Deputy Ratchett. "Do you think your dad would talk to me about coming to Michigan and the life he's built here? I'm looking for someone who came here with nothing and built a good life."

"Maybe. He's a quiet man, doesn't like to talk about himself a lot, but he might go for it. When do you want to talk to him? He's probably working down at the courthouse."

Nick jotted down his cell phone number and told Trixie he would work around her dad's schedule. Then the reporter left the restaurant. It had been a good afternoon.

Chapter 29 — Friday afternoon

J anene printed out her final letter from the work center in the basement under the giant toolshed. She picked it up and read it again. It was short and to the point.

"Pablo: I am writing you this letter to formally absolve you of your debt to me. You are free and clear to leave the farm and find your way. You may take your personal possessions with you, but you must leave all the equipment and tools that belong to the farm. If you decide to stay here and continue working, you must make a new agreement with Juan, who is now in control of this operation. Thank you for all your hard work. Good luck, and may God bless you."

She thought the God bit at the end added a nice touch. Janene signed the letter, then added it to the tall stack of freedom letters, as she thought of them. She had been planning to absolve her workers of their debt since she'd hatched the plan to retire. She liked the idea of riding out on a wave of benevolence. It made her feel good about a business that had evolved into something she was not very proud of. This way, the people who worked for her could strike out on their own or figure out a plan to continue working for Juan. Many were grateful for the opportunity she had given them. Some of the workers she'd become fond of over the years, and a few were so close she considered them almost family and would trust them with anything. Others, she could not stand the sight of and had no faith in whatsoever.

She would divide the freedom letters into separate batches for the nine farms where her workers toiled from sunup to sundown. Her plan was to leave them with employees she trusted for distribution Monday. By then, she would be out of the Thumb and on her way to Port Huron to cross into Canada.

179

Her last farewell would be to Farmer Bud. They had worked together for years and helped each other in numerous ways. Janene had a letter for him and each of the other farmers she contracted with in the Thumb. The letters were similar in nature to the ones she had written the workers—a basic notification that she was turning the operation over to Juan, thanks for the years of success, and a heartfelt but not-too-sappy so-long.

She was proud of what she had accomplished in the early days of her labor consulting business. She'd brought thousands of men and women to the Thumb and helped them get established in their new lives. Her business had also helped hundreds of farmers find the labor they needed to build their agricultural operations.

Satisfaction rushed through her as she headed up the steps to the toolshed to look for Farmer Bud. She needed to talk with him about the work schedule for the rest of the week, the last one she would finalize.

Her good mood did not last beyond the top step. There she came face to face with the farmer and Juan, fear and gloom plain on their faces. Juan spoke first.

"That damn nun is close to dying," he said, pausing to catch his breath. He and Farmer Bud stood with hands on hips, scanning the toolshed to see who might be listening. "My alibi is rock solid, but now we got search parties—Latinos from Bay City and Saginaw—crawling across the Thumb looking for Suzie Alvarez's sister and Maria."

"Okay, we can't do anything about the nun, but what does all this have to do with the two women?" Janene asked. She could see Farmer Bud was not handling the situation well. Sweat washed down from the top of his head, drenching his collar. His chest heaved as he gasped for air. "What did you do with them?"

Juan did not answer. He checked his phone and kept an eye

on Farmer Bud, who was now bent over with his hands on his knees.

"Where are the damn women?"

"Gone. I shipped them off to the hotello in Traverse City," he said. "Jesse and Jake got them tucked away in the nut house tunnels. They are in the process. Nobody searching the Thumb is going to find a trace of them."

The tunnels Juan referred to are the miles of underground passageways originally built for the Traverse City State Hospital in the late 1800s, connecting dozens of buildings on and off the hospital campus. The facility was abandoned in the 1980s but is undergoing a revival. Some of the campus buildings have been repurposed to accommodate shops, restaurants, wineries, and boutiques.

One of the tunnels, which had been blocked off from the rest, led to small storage rooms off campus—and the hotello.

Janene was not impressed. Plus, no one had consulted her about taking the two women captive or moving them across the state.

"Why in the world would you do that?" she asked, incredulous at the idiocy. "Kidnapping them will bring attention to us, dipshit. It's gonna shine a light on what we're doing. We're flying under the radar here, and now you've brought people out to look even closer. I can't think of anything more stupid."

Juan did not appreciate the rebuke, especially in front of Farmer Bud. "You cannot talk to me like that," he said, shaking a thick, stubby finger at her. Janene could see the anger in his eyes. She knew he would take it out on her later, but she did not care. "I am not a child," he said. "I know what I'm doing. Those two bitches were going to cause us nothing but trouble. Now they're gone, and I made it simple. We make money off them, then throw them away just like all the rest."

Janene strode over to the side of the toolshed, where a small business workstation was set up. She grabbed a steel chair and carried it back for Farmer Bud. "Sit your ass down before you croak on us and cause another problem," she said. A foul mood had swept over the redhead. She knew she would have to act fast because these two, she was certain, were not going to help get them out of this jam.

"Okay, here's what we're going to do. Send word out to each of the farms. Tell all the illegals to stop working and go into hiding. We want them to burrow down as if ICE were running right up their asses. Tell them to stay put until the coast is clear. Then get all our legal migrants together and have them fan out to help the search parties. They speak the language. They will know where to look and where not to look. Bonuses for all who help make this go away."

Juan nodded, signaling he understood the directive. Farmer Bud sat with his hands on his knees, though his breathing had slowed almost back to normal. Janene asked him to blink twice if he understood, then twice more if he agreed with the plan.

Instead, Farmer Bud spoke for the first time. "Yes, I like it. We will have a loss in production, but it's okay until this blows over."

Juan said he would spread word of the plan to the other farms. He told Janene he would meet her at her place that evening; she would have some more making up to do for her comments to him. "You will wish you had not called me a dipshit."

Farmer Bud smiled and got up from the chair without speaking.

"One more thing," Janene said. "Both of you better pray for the nun. If she dies, total shit will hit the fan."

Chapter 30 — Late Friday afternoon

Nick flipped through periodicals at the Bad Axe public library, which is located down the street from the Huron County courthouse, the sheriff's department, and the county jail. He checked his cell for the time. Ronaldo Lopez, Trixie's dad, would meet him right after his last landscaping job of the day.

Ronaldo had agreed to talk with Nick as long as his name was not used in any articles or pieces the reporter wrote. The transplanted Cuban had lived in the community for years, and most folks believed he and his wife, Yolanda, had become American citizens. She had—but he had not. Their story was complicated, and Nick was about to find that out.

The reporter put down the copy of *True North Magazine* he'd been reading and gazed outside. It had been cloudy all day, and light rain splashed tiny drops of water on the pavement. Perhaps wet weather would bring Ronaldo's shift to a speedy end, Nick thought. He watched schoolchildren race each other down the sidewalk toward the library. After-school story hour would begin soon.

As the last youngster scooted into the library, he held the door open for an older man with tanned, leathery skin. The man removed his ball cap as he entered the house of books. Nick figured it had to be Ronaldo. He extended his hand, and the two shook and introduced themselves.

The reporter led the landscaper to a lounge area, where they sat in overstuffed chairs almost side by side. In a low voice, Nick told Ronaldo about the story he was developing. He mentioned the tip from Deputy Ratchett and explained how he'd met Trixie at the coffee shop. "I thought your journey to America and the life you've built here would be important to readers of the *Bay City Blade*," he said. "An undocumented worker from this area was killed recently. We're investigating her horrible death but also putting together a reporting project that explores the many facets of immigration. Your story is a positive one that will add context to our reporting."

Ronaldo nodded, but he motioned for Nick to lean closer. "It is way too quiet in here. Let's go back outside—I'm more comfortable outdoors. There's a park down the street. We can skip through the showers."

Nick did not object. An interview is always more productive when the subject feels most comfortable or at ease. Additionally, an outdoor interview would lessen the chances of someone overhearing them.

Ronaldo led the way to City Park. The rain showers had stopped, but they'd left a long line of puddles along the uneven, broken sidewalk. The two hopped and dodged their way to the park. Strangers observing might have thought they were playing a game, but both men were dead serious.

"You cannot reveal my name to anyone," Ronaldo said, pausing to study Nick's face. "I have too much to lose, but what you are working on is important. People need to understand what is going on in their own backyard and why it is happening. If I can help with that, then it's a good thing. But please don't get me deported."

Nick was puzzled. If Ronaldo was a citizen, he asked, why would he worry about deportation?

The two sat across from one another at a picnic table under a tree in a corner of the park, right next to a series of ball fields. Ronaldo nodded toward the courthouse and jail across the street. "Never been in there, and I hope that never changes. I'm trusting you. Don't give me up."

Nick vowed to protect Ronaldo's identity, but he was dying to hear the older man's story. He pulled out his notebook and pen, ready for the landscaper to start at the beginning.

Before Ronaldo could respond, Nick's cell phone dinged with a text message. He reached to shut it off but noticed the note was from Booger: "Figured out your riddle. I know what the message on the dollar bill means. Heading north. Will connect later."

The reporter was delighted, but he had to press ahead with his interview while he had the opportunity to conduct it.

Ronaldo cupped his hands together. He studied them, rubbing both mitts as if tiny needles poked at the joints in his hands. Nick could see his mind had drifted to another time and place. The reporter watched and waited, giving Ronaldo time to collect his thoughts. It was worth the wait.

Ronaldo had grown up in Havana when Fidel Castro was fully in control of Cuba. It was a time of limited freedoms, few economic opportunities, and even less money. As a teenager, Ronaldo lived on the street, looking for any work he could find to help his parents and siblings.

When he first met his future wife, Yolanda, he was smitten. It wasn't long before he and Yolanda had begun to make plans. They wanted a family and a big life together, but they both guessed that was not going to happen in Cuba. They wanted to build a new life in America.

Ronaldo said he inquired about the Cuban flotillas to Miami, which risked all to make it to the shores of South Florida in three to five days, depending on the weather and the US Coast Guard. The floating rafts, often barrels strung together under plywood or assorted planking, were expensive for passage—six thousand dollars for a young man—and extremely dangerous. Over the years, thousands of Cubans had lost their lives in the roiling and wildly unpredictable seas that separated the countries.

For fat fees and liberal, well-placed bribes to local authorities, passage to Mexico could also be purchased. Ronaldo and some friends found an antiques dealer in Havana who arranged to ship them in wooden crates—labeled "Relics, handle with care"—to Tampico, a port city in Tamaulipas, Mexico, and home to the Gulf Cartel, a notorious gang of drug dealers and smugglers who rule the area like the Mafia runs Chicago. The cost of passage? Four thousand dollars each.

It took Ronaldo and Yolanda three years of backbreaking labor in the sugar cane fields to save the money for one passage. The two planned for Ronaldo to make his way to the United States and then send for the love of his life when he'd saved up enough.

Ronaldo and forty other men crossed from Mexico into the United States at Laredo, Texas. They traveled mostly at night, crammed together in the back of a truck with no food and little water. But good fortune smiled on them. They connected with a smuggler who would take them by truck to Houston for a thousand dollars apiece. Yolanda and her family scraped the money together and sent it via Western Union.

In Houston, the young men were able to find help at a shelter run by Catholic Family Services. It was at the shelter, run by nuns and volunteers from the community, that Ronaldo first learned about farm work available in Michigan. Field hands, orchard workers, and dairy help were in big demand. The work was long and hard, but the pay decent and regular.

Ronaldo signed on with a recruiter named Janene, a redhead with a ready smile and comforting words. She promised bonuses, transportation, food, clothing, and a mattress. One of the brochures Janene showed prospective recruits had a photo of a nun with rosy cheeks and wire-rimmed glasses placing a communion wafer on the tongue of a kneeling man with his hands joined together in prayer. The recruits trusted Janene because she was friendly with the nuns, who seemed to like her.

The journey north took a week. They traveled by truck, mostly at night, and stopped at freeway rest areas to use the facilities and stretch.

But the trip was not cheap. Janene had told the Cubans she would keep track of their expenses in her ledger, a thick black book she liked to hold up in front of the men. "Your whole damn lives are right here in this book," she said repeatedly. "I own the book and I own you until your debt is paid in full."

By the time Ronaldo and his traveling companions reached the Thumb of Michigan, they had each run up a tab of fifteen thousand dollars. It took years of living like a hermit and working like a slave for him to save enough money to break away from Janene. He went to work for a Bay County dairy farmer, who eventually helped him bring Yolanda to Michigan. After Trixie was born, they moved back to Huron County, and Ronaldo hooked up with the landscaping company that he still worked for today.

Nick asked if he still kept track of what Janene was doing with the workers in the Thumb.

"That's back when the mega–dairy farms took off," he said, rubbing his hands again. "I knew many of the workers. They wanted to know how to break away from Janene's network. We heard stories about abuse at Janene's farms. It was awful. People were not treated fairly. So-called troublemakers began to disappear."

"You mean they rotated out to work in other parts of Michigan?" Nick asked, stopping to search his pockets for another ink pen when the one he was using dried up. "Where did they go?"

"We lost track of them, like they'd vanished," Ronaldo said. "That's when it got scary. When Juan came into the picture, it was worse. More reports of abuse, more beatings—even torture."

"Did you report it?"

"Who would it be reported to?" he said. A turning car overshot the corner near the park and hit the curb, drawing both men's attention. Ronaldo paused while the driver hopped out and examined his bent wheel. Then he continued. "All these people were here illegally. They had no rights. If they got caught, they lost everything. Instant deportation."

Ronaldo said he had heard that Juan expanded Janene's business by opening up the network to a new line of work: he started accepting bodies.

Nick stopped writing and sat upright. "Bodies from where?"

"All over. They came from everywhere," Ronaldo said. "Juan was smart. He answered this question: What do you do with the body of an illegal immigrant who dies in the United States? People died from farm accidents, car crashes, illnesses, fights, even murder. They had to get rid of the bodies. Burying them, even in the woods, is too dangerous. You don't call the funeral home or the cops. There is no one to call. No family, no relatives. So, you call Juan and he takes care of it. They disappear."

Nick was stunned, trying to absorb Ronaldo's revelation. "Where did the bodies go?" he asked. "What did Juan do with them?"

"That's the big question. Nobody knows. Maybe nobody wants to know."

Nick asked why Ronaldo had not become a citizen. The reporter could see the question had hit Ronaldo hard. His head drooped until his chin rested on his chest. His shoulders sagged. He took a deep breath and let the air slowly escape his lungs. "I killed a man in Ohio," he said, his voice low and remorseful. "It was self-defense. We left the body in a trash can outside a restroom and took off for Michigan. I figured they got my fingerprints and who knows what other evidence, so I didn't try for citizenship."

The confession caught Nick by surprise. He jotted notes, hoping

Ronaldo would continue without prompting.

"I'm only telling you this because Booger says you're okay," he said, straightening as if a tremendous weight had come off his broad shoulders. "Boog stopped by after he left the coffee shop and said you'd be contacting me."

Nick said he understood, and thanked Ronaldo for his candor. He asked if he would share more about the death.

Ronaldo explained that he had been in a fight which ended badly. Another Cuban had attacked him for the small stash of money he had been able to keep during the journey north to Michigan. The fight was over in minutes. Ronaldo's opponent was knocked backward through a porch railing, and one of the splintered spindles went through the man's back between his upper ribs, piercing his heart.

"Only Yolanda knows that story," he said, leaning toward Nick. "She became a citizen, but I didn't because I was afraid the truth would come out about my fight. I couldn't risk it."

The reporter asked how Ronaldo had stayed under the radar all these years.

"I don't vote. I don't own property," he said. "I never complain to the cops or city hall. I work and take care of my family. We have a good life—far better than if I had stayed in Cuba. They would have worked Yolanda to death."

Nick asked where Ronaldo and Yolanda lived if he did not own property.

"My son. He's got half a dozen rentals in the Bad Axe area," he said. "He also bought the landscaping company I work for. My boy turned out to be a good businessman and a good citizen. He's president of the local Lions Club and sits on the Chamber of Commerce. He wants Trixie to work for him, but she's too independent. Wants to be a nurse. She'd be a good one too."

Nick told Ronaldo he'd lived a fascinating life. He thanked him for sharing his story and reaffirmed that Ronaldo's identity would be protected.

The two shook hands again and parted.

When the reporter reached his vehicle, he tried to call Deputy Ratchett, but his cell was busy. Nick was dying to find out about the dollar bill message—and he had new information to share. Juan was in the body disposal business.

Chapter 31 — Friday evening

Deputy Del sauntered up to the front door of what appeared to be an abandoned three-story brick warehouse in Old Town Traverse City. All the windows were blacked out.

Around the corner from the entrance to the hotello, Dave Balz sat in the deputy's 1972 Ford Mustang GT, which he had been instructed to move after the officer gained entry to the establishment. They would stay in touch by text—Del would signal the reporter if he was jeopardized. It was almost dark. Streetlights blinked their way to illumination. The night was about to come alive.

During a stakeout the previous evening, the deputy and Dave had observed taxicabs, limos, shuttles, and private vehicles unloading their passengers after entering an enclosed garage adjacent to the hotello's entrance. A handful of patrons approached the entrance by foot, but no vehicles were parked on the street.

The officer smoothed out any wrinkles that might have creased his tan sports jacket. He wore dark-brown slacks, a white shirt with a button-down collar, and his best pair of cowboy boots, spit-shined to a high amber glow. He thought he had donned the perfect disguise. No one would mistake him for a sheriff's deputy in this city slicker get-up.

He knocked on the door, following the instructions on the back of the free pass he'd received from the Boob Doctor. Two knocks, then pause, then four rapid knocks. A small window in the door opened and a set of harsh eyes looked him up and down. "You a cop?"

"Hell no," Deputy Del said, holding up his pass to chin level so it could be inspected. "I am cleared for takeoff and ready for some fun."

The door swung open. The all-inclusive entry fee of five thousand dollars came out of the deputy's jacket breast pocket, but its origin was the Emmet County Sheriff's Office drug-buy fund. Deputy Del counted out the cash, laid it on the counter, and patted it with his right hand.

Harsh Eyes, who stood six five and weighed in the neighborhood of three hundred pounds—all chiseled muscle—studied the stranger before him. He wore tight faded jeans and a wife-beater that declared "Life is Cherry without the Pits." He pulled the pile of fifties toward him.

At the same time, he handed Deputy Del a one-page list of rules, labeled "The Ten Commandments":

No guns or weapons of any kind.

No fighting unless it's bare knuckles, one on one, in the cage.

No drugs except as provided by the house.

No cheating at cards or games.

No stealing.

No beating the sporting women or men unless you pay for it or they ask for it.

No spitting or splashing of bodily fluids.

No bottle throwing.

No cursing. Patrons must remain civil.

No leaving before dawn—checkout at noon.

Harsh Eyes held out his hand for the deputy's car keys and identification, which he explained could be claimed during checkout in the morning. Del handed over his Michigan driver's license but said he had been dropped at the location by a friend.

The doorman grunted and handed over a basic layout of the club. First floor: bars, restaurants, and live entertainment. Second floor: gambling, sports betting, cage fights, and strippers (female and male). Third floor: bedrooms, group playrooms, and a medical office (with a physician's assistant and nurse on duty). All floors had alcohol and drug dispensaries.

Deputy Del looked over the layout. "Holy moly, don't know where to start. What do you recommend?"

"I suggest you get yourself a drink and roam around. Check the whole place out," Harsh Eyes said. "Take your time, have fun, and pace yourself. Can't tell you the number of guys who come in here, get totally trashed, and pass out by midnight, which is when this place starts to take off."

Good advice, the deputy thought as he moved off toward the bar. It was still early in the evening, but the place was filling up with a variety of customers, many of them married, if a wedding ring on the left hand was still a good indicator.

The main lounge on the first floor looked like a mega–sports bar. Big-screen TVs were strategically positioned high and low on the walls. A different sport played on each television, with the volume muted. "Don't Stand So Close to Me" by the Police blared from unseen speakers, making the lawman chuckle out loud.

Bartenders, both male and female, wore black vests and white ruffled shirts with black bowties. Male and female waitstaff served drinks and food topless. Men wore black dress shorts with black shoes and no socks. Women were dressed in short black skirts with black fishnet stockings and high heels.

Deputy Del was tempted to take a seat at a table, but he was afraid he'd end up with a male waiter. Instead, he stood at a long section of bar with a high footrail but no seats. A waitress approached. The lawman told himself repeatedly to make eye contact and hold it—no matter what.

The waitress, a tall brunette, asked what he'd like to drink. A nametag on her cummerbund told everyone she was Courtney.

"I'm pacing myself, so I think I'll have a Coke on ice—no bourbon just yet," he said, looking past her but keeping his eyes high.

"You a cop?" she asked.

"Hell no," he replied, a bit perturbed at the question. "What makes you think so?'

"Old Spice. Cops always wear Old Spice," she said, smiling. "But don't take it personal. My dad wore Old Spice too."

"Your dad is probably a good guy," he said, trying his best to be friendly, keep the conversation going, and not act like a cop.

"He's dead, but he was a pretty good guy when he was sober," she said, pouring pop from a can over ice. She set the can on the table and stuck her tray under her arm. "But let's talk about you. How'd you find this place? We're not in any of the tourist brochures."

"Got a pass from a buddy. Thought I'd check it out." He sipped from his glass. Courtney was friendly, talkative, and around Suzie's age—which prompted the deputy's next question. "He suggested I look up one of his girlfriends. Do you know Suzie Alvarez?"

The lawman could tell the question surprised her. She didn't respond right away, so he followed up with another along the same lines. He asked if Suzie still worked the top floor.

"Haven't seen her around for a while," she said, wiping the top of the bar with a wet towel in a circular motion that made the deputy blush and look away. "Don't think she's here anymore."

Courtney rushed away to serve another customer, who the deputy thought might be crocked. She handled him like a pro. When he tried to fondle her while she took his order, she slapped him and signaled for a burly bouncer who looked like he ate cement blocks for lunch to drag the groper away.

The deputy sipped at his pop and scanned the cavernous barroom. He'd never imagined such a place, designed to cater to the basest desires of men. But here they were—hundreds of men, all shapes, ages, and races, basking in a den of sin that would have made

Hugh Hefner proud.

Courtney whisked by the deputy and pushed a bar napkin in front of him. He could see writing on it. His hand swallowed the napkin before anyone else at the bar noticed.

After a few moments, Del drained the soft drink and headed for the restroom, where he found an empty stall. He pulled the napkin out of his pocket. "Meet me in the video poker room on the second level in ten minutes. Don't speak with anyone else about Suzie. Your life could be in danger."

Deputy Del read the note again and dropped it in the toilet, signaled the motion detector to flush, and watched the bar napkin swirl away. When it did not pop back up, he left the stall, scanning the area in all directions. He saw no one, but he wondered if a place like this would have cameras inside the restrooms.

The second floor of the hotello offered customers a wide assortment of opportunities to gamble—from old-fashioned poker games to live betting on sporting events to in-house cage fighting. Each room on the second level featured a different event and a different way to lose money. A thousand bucks in tokens was part of the five-thousand-dollar entry fee, but bettors were on their own when the tokens were spent.

Video poker appeared to be the least desirable activity—all the machines were empty. Del walked to the back of the room to make sure he had not missed anyone in the shadows of the dimly lit gambling hall. He wondered if Courtney had set him up, half expecting a couple of the cement block eaters to jump out from between the machines and drag him away. But the place was empty, and he relaxed slightly.

Courtney entered the room and motioned for the deputy to join her at a standing table beside the first machine. During her break period, she had slipped on a loose-fitting jersey with the Detroit

Lions snarling logo on the front.

"We gotta make this quick," she said, glancing back at the doorway. The waitress checked the underside of the table for microphones. "If anybody sees me talking to a cop, I'm toast around here."

"Who says I'm a cop?"

"Aw, come on. You look like a cop, you smell like a cop, you're not drinking alcohol, and you're asking questions about a dead girl who used to work here," she said, her voice rising as she made her point. "You're a cop, and you could end up dead if you talk to the wrong people. This is a place for murder."

The deputy did not reply. He felt stupid for getting busted by the first person he'd had a conversation with at the hotello. But he was lucky to have stumbled upon Courtney, who opened up to him about Suzie.

The waitress talked about meeting the attractive Latina, who had befriended Courtney when she first walked into the place. Suzie didn't want Courtney to end up on her path, urging her to get out as soon as she could.

"I shoulda followed her advice, but no use crying about it now," she said, checking the entrance again. Courtney moved in toward the deputy and kept her voice low. "When they brought Suzie here from across state, they put her on the needle. They hooked her on heroin. Only way she could feed the habit was working the third floor. That's how most of the women are started here."

"Okay, she was doing what they wanted and she was making them money, so what happened?" he asked, trying to make sense of why she'd been be killed. "Was she stealing from them, or what?"

"I'm not sure. Suzie was smart. She figured out what they were doing." The young woman stepped away from the table and walked out into the hallway to make sure they were still alone. A solo customer was approaching, she said, so she spoke quickly when she returned. "She told me it had something to do with the farms in the Thumb, some new business based on the labor network they had going. She said a guy named Juan was running it."

After a few moments, the loner she had spotted in the hallway entered the video poker parlor—middle-aged, slender, and dressed in expensive casual clothes. Enough gold chains hung from his neck to open a pawnshop. Courtney continued chatting, but now she was telling Del about the place as if she were a tour guide.

Gold Chains sipped clear liquid with a lime from a rock glass, swirling ice and looking over the video poker games. About halfway down the hall, he pulled up and then sat down in front of a flashing, whirling machine. Del relaxed.

"Really, that's all I know," Courtney said, still rattled by the stranger's presence. "All of a sudden, Suzie disappeared. I figured they rotated her out to work one of the other hotellos. Then I heard they found her in the back of a pickup truck. I cried all day."

The deputy asked Courtney if he could call her later when she was not working. The waitress balked at the request, pointing her chin toward a recording device in a nearby corner. She whispered she would contact him later. "Do I call the state police or the sheriff's department to find you?"

"Sheriff. Ask for Del," he said quietly. He turned to check on Gold Chains, who appeared engrossed by the machine he was feeding tokens. The deputy decided he should leave the den of sin sooner rather than later, because his civilian disguise wasn't really fooling anyone. "How do I get out of this place before dawn? The guy at the big wooden door has my ID."

"Only way out is a medical emergency," she replied. "And they won't give you a refund."

Deputy Del nodded and thanked her. He also urged her to find new employment right away.

"You don't want to be here when we bust this place," he said. "Besides, you're too nice to be in a shit hole like this. Got a daughter about your age. You gotta get out of here."

Courtney smiled and patted the cop on his forearm. She left the video poker room first. He waited several minutes, then made his way back down to the entryway.

Just before he reached the table and chair set up for Harsh Eyes, the lawman cried out in agony, clutched his chest with both hands, staggered three steps, and flopped to the floor.

The doorman raced to Del's side.

"It's the big one," the officer said, gasping for air. The doorman's eyes suddenly looked soft, concerned. Del held his chest while convulsing on the floor. "I need help. Gotta call 911."

The doorman told him not to do that until the house medical staff got him outside. Then he would be on his own.

Outside, the medical attendant leaned him up against a streetlight and hustled back inside the hotello, banging the door closed behind him. The deputy continued acting and staggered down the street, briefly stopping at each light post.

Finally he signaled Dave to bring the Mustang around. Once inside, Del raised his hand for Dave to high-five. "Man, have I got some shit to tell you!"

They drove off into the night.

Chapter 32 — Friday night

Monica waited by the doorway with a bucket in her right hand, trying to control her breathing while she waited for the Hulk, the nickname she'd given the large, shadowy figure who came to her cell to check on her.

Of course, she had no way to keep track of time, but she guessed that the Hulk clip-clopped down the hallway, stopped to open another cell—presumably to check on a second captive—and then came to her door every two or three hours.

The sounds were distinctive. She memorized them, right down to the turning of the lock. She had also memorized the number of steps in each direction from the open doorway.

With nothing but time on her hands, Monica next choreographed the movements she would make once she heard the lock turn. In her mind, it would be easy, like dancing. But now, as she waited for the Hulk, her heart raced and her mind clicked through every possible way that things could go horribly wrong.

Monica was counting on two things for her plan to work: surprise and swift action. The Hulk was predictable, like a machine. The door would swing open, and he would use his flashlight to locate and blind her. Then he would check her buckets and back out of the room, with the clank of the lock the final act of his visit. Monica would have to move like lightning—and flawlessly. She was also hoping that the few seconds of confusion when he opened the door and could not locate her would give her eyes a chance to adjust to the sudden light.

Finally, off in the distance came the sound of his boots on the hard floor. They stopped at the cell before hers, as always, and she heard the lock clank. Then his voice, but this time she didn't hear the faint voice of whoever was in the other cell, which worried her. Monica hoped the woman wasn't injured or ill. If Monica's plan worked, she was determined to rescue the other captive too, who she hoped was Maria.

The lock clanked again, a chilling sound. He was coming.

Clip-clop, *clip-clop*. The Hulk was moving toward her. In eighteen steps, he would be standing outside her door. Monica waited and counted, her heart pounding, her breathing ragged but low.

When the Hulk stopped, she could hear him fumbling with his keys. His breathing was congested, as if he had allergies or a cold.

It seemed like an hour to Monica, but it was only a moment before her lock clinked and the door swung open. The Hulk stepped into the cell and swept the room with his flashlight.

Monica stood behind the opened door, blinking furiously to adjust to the brightness of the flashlight. When she saw his light was aimed at the far end of the cell, she sprang into action, slamming the door into the Hulk's right side as hard as she could. Before he could steady himself, she stepped out from behind the door, planted both feet, and swung the bucket by its handle with all the force her arms could muster. The bucket hit him in the head, knocking him sideways into the doorway. In three steps, just as she'd practiced, she swung her knee up and planted it firmly in his groin.

The Hulk howled in agony, crashing to the floor. But Monica was not finished. She slammed the bucket down over his head. It was then she noticed a large dent in the side of the pail, a result of its initial introduction to his face. She grinned at that. With the bucket covering his head and the Hulk's shoulders leaning against the doorway, Monica banged the bucket into the wooden doorframe four times in rapid succession.

The Hulk was had. Monica dragged him by his feet further into the cell. He sprawled on the floor, still clutching his groin and moaning, barely moving. She grabbed his flashlight and noted the keys were still in the lock, then patted his pockets for a weapon. He was unarmed.

Monica stepped back and scanned the room with the flashlight to find the source of the dripping water that had tormented her since she regained consciousness. The *plunk, plunk, plunk* came from a leaking pipe that ran along the ceiling at the back of the room.

When she swung the light across the front of the cell, she spotted writing on the wall. Instantly she burst into tears. There above the doorway, written on the wall with coal, was the full message Suzie had been trying to convey near her bunk at the calf barns and sewn into her waistband: "*Más allá del puente, se encuentran los cuerpos*" or "Beyond the bridge, you will find bodies."

Monica wiped tears from her cheeks and gulped for air. No time for sentiment, she thought. She checked the Hulk again, who had rolled to his other side. Then she stepped around him and pulled the cell door shut, turning the lock and pulling the keys.

The Hulk screamed, "Don't leave me, please."

The desperate plea did not slow or sway her. Monica moved quickly, using the flashlight to lead her to the next cell. She could see that the oval tunnel was made of bricks and stretched off well past the end of her light. When she got to the cell she believed the Hulk had been visiting, she opened the lock, feeling lucky that the same key worked in this door too.

The flashlight revealed Maria stretched out on the floor. Monica squealed in delight. But Maria did not react to the sound or the light. She was not moving at all.

Monica jumped to her side and checked her pulse, then listened for the sound of breathing. Both were faint.

"Maria, Maria," she said, trying to lift the young woman's head and shoulders. "We've got to get out of here. Can you get up? Can you walk?"

Maria did not respond, but she did moan. Monica used the flashlight to check her body for injury. That's when she discovered needle marks and blood on both arms. Maria had been drugged, which made Monica's blood boil. She was more determined than ever to take Suzie's friend with her.

"Come on, work with me," Monica said, standing and lifting the young woman to her knees. Maria clutched her arm, but weakly, and the two women stood and lurched into the wall. But they did not go back down, which Monica believed was progress. They stood together a moment. Maria moaned again and tried to speak, but her words were garbled.

Monica was afraid to leave Maria behind—no telling how long it would be before the Hulk was missed and someone would start looking for him.

"Okay, we've got to move. I lost a brother who died for this country, and a sister who lost her life trying to stay here. I am not going to lose you. Let's go, Maria." Limping along together, the two women somehow made it out into the tunnel, though Monica had no idea which way to go. Dim lights lit the long hallway in both directions. She decided to go in the opposite direction from which the Hulk came to make his cell checks.

They staggered down the tunnel together toward where the passage turned, then divided in two directions. Off in the distance, she could hear music playing—what she thought was classic rock 'n' roll. They followed their ears.

The music was coming from behind a door that looked very much like the ones to their cells. Monica put her ear to the door, but the only sound she could hear was blaring rock music. She pulled at the door. It was locked.

Monica balled up her fist and banged on the door, hoping rescuers would step out and save them. No response. She leaned Maria against the wall next to the door and pounded on the door again. This time the music stopped and the door opened.

It was Juan.

"Welcome to the hotello, ladies," he said, grabbing Monica by the hair to pull her into the entryway. Maria fell down onto the floor. Juan dragged her in too and dropped her in front of Monica. "Come right on in and join the party."

Chapter 33 — Saturday morning

Nick tried to call Deputy Ratchett on his cell phone with no luck. When the reporter checked in with the newsroom of the *Bay City Blade*, he discovered that he had two new messages: another from Booger and one from Dave, who was still working with Deputy Del.

Ratchett's note was succinct. "Meet me at the abandoned marina northwest of Rogers City. Called in the Coast Guard. Your story is about to blow wide open. Hustle your butt up here. –Boog."

Dave asked for a return call as soon as Nick was free. The C-Man also wanted an update from Nick. Specifically: did Nick have a fresh story on Suzie Alvarez or her missing sister for Sunday's morning edition of the *Blade*?

Good question, Nick thought. Maybe—it depended on what the reporter would be able to pull together from Dave, the two sheriff's deputies they had been working with, the Mexican Mafia search party, and ICE Agent Stevens. He decided to follow the advice of Deputy Ratchett and head north quickly.

Nick did not stop in Bay City on his way Up North. He pushed the Firebird across town as fast as he could, and when he hit the northbound lane of I-75, it was full speed ahead to Rogers City, located near the top of Michigan's Lower Peninsula and just southeast of Mackinaw City.

As Nick reached for his cell to return Dave's call, it rang. Caller ID revealed that Tanya was trying to reach him. Guilt surged through him. Other than the visit to the hospital bed of Sister S., he had not spent much time with her since the proposal, and he knew she wanted to set a date for their wedding. Nick had been so consumed with working the story, he simply had not had time to even consider a wedding date. But he did not want Tanya to think he was getting cold feet. He thought about letting the call go to voicemail but did not want to miss the chance to talk with her either. Nick answered on the fourth ring.

"Hi, Tanya, what's up?"

"Oh, Nick, it's not good," Tanya said. Nick could hear the stress in her voice, and his mind accelerated through the possibilities. Had she been threatened? Did she have a close call? Had there been another accident? "It's Sister S. She's taken a turn for the worse. She's really struggling."

Bad news, but Nick was relieved that Tanya's well-being was not in question. He sighed quietly. "Is she having complications?" he asked.

"Heavy congestion. They're afraid her heart might fail. Nick, the docs told the nuns staying with her to call for a priest. They want to give her the Last Rites."

The sacrament of Extreme Unction, or the final anointing of the body, is offered to Catholics who are gravely ill. Nick knew that anyone who gets Last Rites is usually on their way to final check-out.

"Oh no!" Nick told Tanya he was on his way to Rogers City to meet Booger, who had a break in the case. But he agonized about heading north while the nun might be on her way out the door.

"It's okay, Nick," Tanya said. "Stay on the story—that's what Sister S. would want. Help bring the bastards to justice. There's nothing you can do here. We're keeping the rosaries going. Finish the job you set out to do, but be careful out there."

Wow, Nick thought, that was why he loved this woman.

The reporter still had difficulty saying those words out loud, but since his feelings for her had become so profound, he opened his mouth and the words spilled out with surprising ease. "I love you, Tanya."

It helped that no one was with him in the Firebird when he pronounced his love, but he was delighted that he could say it because he knew it would make her happy too.

"As soon as I get finished with this story, we'll make plans for the wedding," he said. "I promise. We'll set the date in stone and make it happen. Just let me wrap this story up and put a bow on it."

After they hung up, Nick tried calling Dave. His cell was busy. He tried to check in with the Garcias to see if the search parties had had any luck locating Monica or Maria. Again, nothing, so he left a voice message.

It was hot and sunny out. The reporter rolled down his driver's-side window and let the warm air rush through the Firebird. Nick inhaled slowly, pulling the fresh air into his lungs, and it lifted his spirits despite the intense pressure. He had never worked on a story where so many people who had helped him were now in jeopardy. The health and future of Sister S. was in question—and she was such a sweet woman. What was her crime, he thought, other than trying to help him and Monica? And now both Maria and Monica had disappeared—poof, gone, missing without a trace.

As Nick passed West Branch on his way to Rogers City, his cell phone rang. It was Dave, who was giddy with excitement about his experience at the hotello.

"Hi, Dave. What happened at the hotello? I am dying to know!"

"I didn't go in, on orders from the C-Man, but Deputy Del did." Dave's exuberance dragged Nick out of his funk. He pushed down the accelerator and kicked the Firebird well past the speed limit. Dave often had the same effect on Nick. "Incredible," Dave said. "From his description, it's unlike anything we've ever experienced.

Massive whorehouse with all the bells and whistles. Lights, music, and neon in one big old building like it's the Vegas strip."

"Right, like most people have never experienced or even heard of, for that matter," Nick said. "You've got to sit down and write a story about the place as told to you by Deputy Del. Get lots of detail and color. Pump him dry of information. It will make a great sidebar."

"For when? When are we publishing?" Dave asked. "I got a full report from him last night after we left the hotello. Took careful notes, but I've only talked to him briefly today. I think he's getting ready to bust the place."

"Sunday, we might publish Sunday, depending on what happens in Rogers City. We're getting close. I'm meeting Booger—almost there now. He says he's got the dollar bill code figured out."

Road construction on I-75 had narrowed traffic from three lanes to two. Nick slowed the Firebird to keep pace with the rest. He steered with one hand and held his cell and connection to Dave with the other.

Dave explained that Deputy Del was meeting with the Grand Traverse County sheriff and county prosecutor. The Emmet County lawman had told his counterparts from the Traverse City area that it was imperative they act today.

"He said he met a young woman at the hotello named Courtney," Dave said. "She reminded him of his daughter. He's worried about her getting in trouble. Told her to quit and get out, but he wants to make sure she's safe."

"I think you're starting to like Deputy Del," Nick said. "Glad we connected with him."

Dave agreed. It wasn't often that his initial impressions of news sources were wrong, but he grudgingly admitted the deputy was a great find. "Yeah, I gotta give him credit. We got lucky with him on this case. He's a walking cliché when it comes to northern Michigan law enforcement, but he's also one hell of a guy. When this is all over, he's going to take me out fishing on Lake Michigan. We'll get a cooler full of beer and have some fun."

The reporters laughed at the idea of relaxing. They were both ready for a break, but not until they wrapped the story. They agreed to stay in touch hourly through the rest of the day.

Before Nick clicked off, he told Dave about Sister S. getting the Last Rites. Tanya and the nuns, led by Sister P., were praying up a storm, he said. And he'd heard nothing new from the search parties looking for Monica and Maria out in the Thumb. It looked bleak. He worried for the fate of all three women. But the fact that so many lives had been threatened, including his own, also told Nick how big a story they were developing. Powerful people with access to lots of money were desperate to push them off their trail.

The Firebird cleared the last orange barrel, and Nick gunned the big V-8. Rogers City was less than an hour away. He decided to try Booger's cell again, but he'd entered an area with no service. Nick tossed his cell in the bucket seat next to him, grabbed the steering wheel with both hands, and pushed down the accelerator. He wasn't concerned about getting a speeding ticket. He was chasing a great story at high speed—and nothing else mattered.

* * *

When Nick pulled off I-75, he started looking for the landmarks Booger had mentioned in his message. The abandoned marina, he knew from reading *True North Magazine*, was located between Rogers City and Cheboygan. It had been carved out of the earth with dynamite and heavy equipment in the 1950s when an upstart mining company tried to make money shipping limestone out of the area.

But the upstart was competing with a Belgium-based global mining company that had operated the world's largest limestone quarry near Rogers City since the early 1900s. It wasn't long before the newcomers realized they had way more ambition than money or investors. Within three years, the company went belly-up, pulling out of northeast Michigan and leaving an unfinished marina in its wake. Since then, the marina had pretty much sat empty, except for occasional boaters looking for a secluded place to party.

A high cliff just off the highway overlooked the southwest corner of the marina. Nick found the turnoff and spotted a Huron County Sheriff's Office cruiser parked in the shade of a half-dozen seventy-foot oaks. He left the Firebird next to the patrol car, pulled his 35mm camera with its high-powered zoom lens out of the trunk, and looked for Deputy Ratchett.

Booger was stretched out on his belly in the grass near the edge of the cliff. Without speaking, Nick moved in close to the deputy.

"'Bout time you got here," Booger said, refusing to look away from the binoculars he had trained on the harbor. "Gol-durned good thing too, because the show is about to begin."

"Hey, I burned up the highway getting here," Nick said. He could see a solitary boat in the marina, tied to a makeshift dock. Two figures appeared to be loading the back end of the boat. "What's going on down there?"

Booger handed over the binoculars reluctantly, telling Nick to check out the captain, the taller of the two loading the boat. The reporter focused the binoculars on the watercraft first and caught a glimpse of the boat's name: *Empty Pockets*. Then he recognized Captain Ned.

Deputy Ratchett reached into his shirt pocket for the slip of paper with the numbers and letters from the dollar bill he had copied. Booger had rearranged the characters to read "Ned MC56789TL

EP."

"Do you see it now?" the deputy asked.

Nick did. "EP" stood for *Empty Pockets*, and the remaining numbers and letters were the boat's identification number.

"You got it. Took me a while, but I kept playing with different sequences until it fell into place and made sense," Booger said, a smile consuming his face at the accomplishment. "I ran right up to Grindstone City, but Ned had already skedaddled. One of the guys he charters with told me about this old marina. It was a hunch, but my gut told me to get Up North, and here we are."

Nick handed back the binoculars and set up his camera. He snapped several shots of the boat, the men, their cargo, and the covered pickup truck that they were unloading. He also took photos of a large refrigerated truck that was parked in the tall weeds off to the side of the main entryway, all its windows and doors wide open. The lettering on the side indicated the truck was used to distribute food, which made Nick wonder why it was sitting in an abandoned marina.

Deputy Ratchett peered through the binoculars at the activity near *Empty Pockets*. "What do you suppose the cargo is—what are they haulin'?"

Nick hesitated before answering, then spat it out. "Don't know for sure, of course, but my guess is those are bodies they're loading onto the boat."

Booger dropped the binoculars, half rising from his prone position. "Bodies? What kind of bodies?"

"The dead kind," Nick said, then tried to explain. He told the deputy he could not reveal his source, but he'd interviewed a man who had come through Janene's labor network. "He said they expanded their service—doing body disposal. Those blue tarps they're lugging around look like bodies to me."

"Well, I'll be a coon dog's flea," the deputy said. "Why would they take bodies?"

Nick aimed his 35mm at the men loading the boat and snapped off another dozen images. "They found a niche that needed filling," he said. "And it fits right in with the other message Suzie left behind. She wrote, 'Beyond the bridge'—couldn't read the rest, but I'm willing to bet Ned is going to haul those bodies beyond the bridge for disposal. We just don't know where."

The two men on the boat had finished their work. The shorter one returned to his pickup truck. Ned started the boat and let the engine idle.

Deputy Ratchett told Nick that a Coast Guard boat was anchored off Bois Blanc Island, called Bob-Lo by the locals, waiting for his signal to move in and close off the entrance to the marina.

Nick hurried down toward the marina entrance with his camera while Booger hopped in his cruiser to pull over the driver of the pickup truck. Soon, Ned and his accomplice would be in custody.

The cell phone in Nick's pocket dinged with a text from Dave. "Get over to Traverse City ASAP. Deputy wants to bust the hotello, but the bigshots want him to do it before the high rollers—bankers, lawyers, judges, politicians, real estate brokers, business owners, celebrities, and editors—show up and take over the place tonight. Hustle up. This is going to be fun."

Dave's alert gnawed at Nick. Should he stay and get photos of the arrest of Captain Ned, he wondered, or shoot to Traverse City and try to record the raid of the hotello, which might include the apprehension of famous people and community big shots? What a dilemma!

Nick sprinted to his Firebird. It was nearly eleven o'clock now, and a two-and-a-half-hour run along M-68 from Rogers City to Traverse City would get him there just in time for the bust. He sent

Booger a text message that an urgent development in the case had arisen and he was on his way to Traverse City. He would call the deputy later to find out what was learned from Captain Ned and the cargo aboard *Empty Pockets*.

Chapter 34 — Saturday morning

Monica awoke to the sound of water dripping again, but this time she could see the source of it. She and Maria were handcuffed together and chained to a wall in some kind of utility room. Their mouths were sealed with duct tape. The drip came from a leaking pipe underneath a large sink.

Both women lay on the floor. Maria's eyes were open, but she was motionless. Monica's last recollection was of being dragged through a doorway by Juan, then kicked. Her head ached. She could see needle marks on her arm, like Maria's.

Monica used her free forearm to work back the duct tape from her lips. She whispered to Maria, "Are you hurt? Can you move?"

Maria shifted her body and sat upright. She scraped away a corner of the duct tape too and whispered that she was okay. She breathed deeply, exhaling as the two women checked out their surroundings.

A single dim light bulb dangled from the ceiling near the back of the small room. A short workbench with an assortment of hand tools was attached to the wall underneath the light. If she could just get to that bench and the tools, Monica figured they might get free again. But the handcuffs biting into her right wrist told her it was not going to be easy.

She listened for sounds coming from outside the utility room. Nothing. Silence.

In the corner of the room to the right of the door rested a broom and a dust mop. Monica motioned to Maria that she wanted to try and reach them. The two women stretched out on the floor as far as their tether would let them.

Monica, who was closest to the corner, lifted her leg and tried to catch the dust mop handle with her toe. She missed it by inches, so she tried again. Same result. In a low voice, she urged Maria to stretch and pull as far as possible.

This time Monica's toe grazed the mop handle. She tried once more, straining so hard she grunted out loud. The mop handle dislodged and landed on the floor next to Monica with a loud smack.

"Yes!" Maria cried out. Immediately Monica put a finger to her lips.

"Okay," Maria whispered, "sorry."

They lay motionless, listening for anyone outside the utility room who might have heard the bang. Silence.

Monica sat up and stretched again, using the mop handle in her fully extended arm to knock down the broom. Then, with the broom and dust mop in hand, Monica laid them end to end, overlapping the handles by about six inches. She tore the duct tape off her face and used it to bind the handles. Maria did the same.

Monica tested the bound handles. Super strong.

The broom and mop gave Monica about eight feet of reach. She held the broom straw in one hand and extended the swivel head on the dust mop up to the workbench, where she swept pole sideways. Tools rattled but did not come down. Her shoulder ached. She swept the bench again. Screwdrivers fell first, then an adjustable wrench, then a hammer. Silently Monica prayed for a hacksaw, but there was none.

Next she pulled the tools within reach, trying to figure out how she could best use them. A large flathead screwdriver would substitute for a chisel. Monica whispered to Maria to stretch out the links of the handcuffs that connected the women to a large steel ring bolted to the wall. Three whacks of the hammer on the makeshift chisel broke the handcuff links. The women had freed themselves, but complete escape would prove more challenging.

Monica studied the room's single door. It looked sturdy, with a deadbolt lock and steel hinges and no window. She considered using the hammer and screwdriver to chisel out the center pin holding the hinges together but was afraid the banging would be too loud.

The women moved the boxes stored around the sides of the room and located a vent for the heating and cooling system's cold air return. If they could squeeze into the vent, Monica figured, they might be able to make their way to another room that was not locked. A Phillips screwdriver removed the vent cover. Monica stuck the screwdriver in the waistband of her shorts, and within minutes they were crawling on their bellies in the ductwork.

After what seemed an eternity of wriggling through the cramped, dark space, the women came to a T in the ductwork. Monica led the way, which took them to a vent cover opening to an office. The vent was positioned just above floor level. The room was dark and empty except for business furnishings.

Monica used a corner of her T-shirt to pinch the pointed end of one of the screws and twist it clockwise until it loosened. By the time she'd loosened all four screws, her fingers were bleeding, but she and Maria had a way out. The women squeezed through and dropped about a foot to the floor headfirst.

Maria wanted to try the office phones and call 911. She reached for the receiver, but Monica grabbed her hand in midair.

"And what would we tell them? We have no idea where we are," Monica said. "Plus, it's a business line. Others will see the line light up, and people—bad people—will come looking for us. Let's not try the phones until we know more."

Maria nodded in agreement, but Monica could see the disappointment in her face.

"I just want to get out of here," Maria said, her eyes welling up.

"If we don't, they're going to kill us just like they did Suzie. Let's try the door."

Monica turned the doorknob, which was unlocked. The women's eyes met. She pushed the door an inch and peeked outside—nothing in sight.

Maria took a deep breath. "Let's go. I say we take the risk."

They pushed the door open and stepped out into the hallway. A lone figure stood leaning against the wall, clapping his hands slowly.

Monica's heart sank. Maria cried out. They froze in their tracks like a couple of stone statues.

"I gotta give you credit," Juan said, a big smile on his face. "You are two tough, snot-nosed bitches, but it's time for you to go into a cage."

But behind Juan, a woman was creeping up on her tiptoes. Maria and Monica did not acknowledge her, and when the newcomer was a few feet behind Juan, she ran the final three steps and leaped onto his back before he could turn around. It was Courtney, and she used her fingernails to rip at his eyes in each direction.

"Make that that three tough, snot-nosed bitches!" With her legs wrapped around him and her hands tearing at his face, Courtney rode Juan like a horse.

Juan bent over, trying to protect his eyes and shake the crazy person who would not let go. He staggered and slammed sideways into the cement block wall. Monica and Maria dove at the back of his knees like linebackers taking down a running back. He crashed to the floor, where all three women pummeled him. Then Monica pulled the screwdriver from the waistband of her shorts and jammed it into the front of his thigh. Juan howled in agony.

Maria ran back into the office and yanked the telephone and its cord from the nearest desk. She used the line to bind Juan's hands behind his back and his feet at the ankles, leaving him hogtied and writhing on the floor. Courtney would not let go of him. Monica stood and backed away from the two on the floor.

"Who are you?" Monica asked the third woman, her breathing labored. Maria joined her after finishing the last of Juan's knots.

Courtney stood and kicked Juan before she retreated to where Maria and Monica were watching. "I'm the only friend your sister Suzie had in this place. I felt horrible when she disappeared. Last night I heard Suzie's sister had been brought here through the tunnels, so I came back this morning to see if I could find you in the building. You look just like her."

Monica hugged Courtney, and Maria began to cry. The three women had loved Suzie, and now they had united to defeat the bastards who took her down. They huddled together over Juan to savor the moment.

But Monica was not finished. She went to work on Juan. She kneeled down beside him and grabbed the screwdriver handle, twisting it slightly. "Juan, who killed my sister?"

"Don't know, don't care."

"Wrong answer," she said, pushing the screwdriver in until the tool wedged in his thighbone. Juan screamed as his leg jerked. "One more time, who killed my sister?"

"Santa Claus. The Easter Bunny. I have no idea, now get away from me, you nasty bitch."

"Wrong answer again," she said, leaning on the screwdriver handle. Juan screamed louder and groaned this time. "You know, I can do this all afternoon if you want, or you can tell me what I came to Michigan to find out. Who killed Suzie?"

"Okay, okay, I did—and I enjoyed watching her die," he said, gasping for air and trying to break free. "Now get away from me."

Why had Suzie been buried and exhumed? Monica turned the

screwdriver handle again. Juan jerked violently on the floor.

"Fine! I was pissed because she discovered what we were doing with the bodies, so I killed her and buried her," he said, gulping air as if that would take away the pain. "But Janene insisted we dig her up and dump her with the others. Would have all worked out, but that damn pickup truck broke down on the way to the marina."

Monica turned the screwdriver sideways and pushed until it came out the other side, bringing muscle, flesh, and blood with it. Juan passed out, but Monica stood up and screamed at him.

"I knew it was you, you son of a bitch, and I could kill you right now without blinking an eye! But I want to see you rot in prison for the rest of your miserable life."

Courtney grabbed Monica's arm and urged her to let it go for now. "Had a cop in here last night asking about Suzie," she said. "He's coming back with warrants and an army of cops to bust this place, but I have no idea when. We need to get out of the building before Juan's thugs come looking for him."

The three women dragged Juan into the office, leaving a trail of blood that Maria wiped up with a piece of Juan's shirt. By now he was regaining consciousness, moaning and squirming against his bindings, so Monica decided to gag him with a rolled-up newspaper. When he refused to open for insertion of the newspaper roll, she stuck a pencil in his left butt cheek. He cried out again, and she crammed the paper in his mouth, using more telephone line to wrap around his head and hold the newspaper roll firmly in his pie hole.

"Follow me," Courtney said. "We'll have to move slowly and be quiet, but I know how to get to the parking lot from here."

The three women left Juan tied up and gagged on the floor behind a desk. Maria asked to kick him again on the way out, but Monica said she wanted the pleasure, delivering a swift shot to his groin. Maria and Courtney could not resist the opportunity. They both gave him a parting kick to the privates, and Maria spit on him as they left.

"You wanted to turn us into prostitutes, making money on our backs," Maria said. "But look who is on his back now, you bastard!"

The three snot-nosed ladies filed out. Monica turned out the lights to the office and locked the doorknob from the inside. It was just after one in the afternoon.

Chapter 35 – Saturday afternoon

Nick pulled up at the hotello in Traverse City just as police were leading resort employees in handcuffs out of the building.

The whole area was cordoned off with yellow tape. Streets in each direction were blocked by a variety of official vehicles, their lights flashing: the Michigan State Police, the county sheriff's department, city cops, and ICE.

The reporter was disappointed he had missed the beginning of the raid. But Dave had not missed a moment. Deputy Del had made sure Dave had a safe but front-row seat to the action.

"Hi, Nick," Dave said, a broad smile on his face. "I got it all documented, including photos. I especially love the one with the cops knocking down the front door with a battering ram. So cool!"

Nick clapped his hands at the news, more enthusiastic than ever to get back to Bay City to put their reporting project together. "I called the C-Man on the way here—he's pulling together a team of editors, photographers, designers, and a graphic artist to meet us. Where are the TV news crews? Did they already leave?"

Dave beamed. It was shaping up to be a great day for the *Blade* team, and he basked in the limelight. "Deputy Del assured me they would not be called until the arraignments are scheduled," he said. "He knows this is our story. We're getting it exclusively."

While the reporters talked, Nick noticed an ambulance not far from the front entrance of the hotello. When an EMT opened the rear door, he could see Monica, Maria, and another woman sitting inside receiving treatment.

"Monica!" Nick yelled as he raced toward the ambulance. "Monica! I'm so glad you're okay."

All three women looked up to see who was shouting. Monica recognized Nick's voice and pushed the ambulance door wider.

Though she was attached to an IV drip, she dragged it with her as she stepped down from the vehicle to greet the reporter.

Nick hugged her. Monica began to cry. "I thought we were done for, Nick," she said. "Maria and I were kept in a dungeon. We escaped and got caught, and then we escaped again. I can't believe we made it. Suzie had to be watching out for us from above."

"You've got to tell us the whole story," Nick said. "We had no idea what happened to you. Search teams from Bay City were crawling all over the Thumb looking for you and Maria. Couldn't find a thing."

Monica sobbed on Nick's shoulder. He patted her back gently as she told him they'd done it. "Juan killed Suzie," she said, still crying. "We did it. We found out what happened to her."

Nick was impressed. He asked how she'd gotten that information.

"I applied the right amount of pressure and he spilled his guts," she said, her spirits rising as she wiped away tears. "Juan confessed freely and openly. He said he killed Suzie and buried her."

"Bastard!"

Nick asked about the other woman in the ambulance.

"Her name is Courtney. She was Suzie's friend and helped us break free. After what we've been through, we're sisters for life! Speaking of sisters, what's the latest on Sister S.? Is she doing okay after the crash?"

Nick updated her, saying the doctors had suggested calling a priest to give the Last Rites. He could see that the news upset Monica, who stepped back into the ambulance to tell Maria, who loved Sister S. as if she were an adopted mother. The two women hugged and Maria wiped away tears.

"Where is Sister S.? Maria wants to see her as soon as possible," Monica said.

"St. Mary's in Saginaw. You better hurry."

Chapter 36 – Sunday morning

Nick walked down to the front step of his apartment building to pick up his copy of the Sunday *Bay City Blade*. Though he was dressed only in his underwear and a robe, he paused to admire the front page, which was completely devoted to the story he and Dave had developed.

As the reporter studied page one, a neighbor drove by and hollered out his window, "Hey, Nick! Put some pants on, will ya—you're scaring the kids. And quit scratchin' yourself while you read. It's unbecoming. By the way, good stories!"

Nick waved at the neighbor and thanked him, but he stayed put to devour the story. The main photo on the front page showed several oblong objects wrapped in blue tarp and chains, believed to be bodies being loaded onto *Empty Pockets*, Captain Ned's charter boat. The article ran beside and underneath the picture.

A second article by Dave Balz detailed the nefarious activities at the hotello, as told to the reporter by Deputy Del and Courtney. It appeared next to a photo of the front door of the hotello being knocked down at the beginning of the raid. The article and photo were accompanied by the hotello's Ten Commandments—the rules of the house—and a detailed drawing showing how the hotello was laid out, floor by floor.

Both articles were accompanied by a dozen more photos and jumped to full inside pages of the A section of the *Blade*.

For Monday's edition of the paper, Nick had written a profile piece about Monica and her quest to find her sister's killer. It included sidebar articles about Maria and Sister S. and their ordeals. The nun, who had stabilized but remained in a coma, was still in question.

Doctors said they weren't sure if she would ever recover fully. The package was complete with photos of all three women.

For Tuesday's paper, Nick and Dave planned to write profile articles on Janene and Juan, detailing how they had established and kept secret their labor network for undocumented workers in the Thumb. The package would include an article about dairy farming operations and the demand for labor in the Thumb and across Michigan. Graphic artists had turned the vigilantes' Wanted poster into a main art element, accompanied by an article detailing what the reporters had learned about the people who created the flyers. Its headline: "ICE – Poster mostly bluster by anonymous tuffs."

It was a ton of work, but it was reporting that Nick was proud of. He folded up the paper, stuck it under his arm, and took it inside for Tanya to review. When he reached the kitchen table, he just had to read the main article again:

Human trafficking ring busted, underwater graveyard discovered after Blade probe
By *Nick Steele and Dave Balz*
Blade *reporters*

An investigation by the *Bay City Blade* revealed that Suzie Alvarez, an undocumented immigrant whose body was found in the back of a pickup truck in northern Michigan last week, was killed to protect the secrecy of an underwater graveyard located just north of Mackinac Island.

Today, the US Coast Guard is pulling the bodies of hundreds of unidentified persons, thought to be undocumented immigrants, out of a three-hundred-foot-deep cavern in Lake Huron between Mackinac, Goose, and Bois Blanc islands. On Saturday authorities arrested Ned Jurgens, a charter boat captain, who was about to dump four bodies wrapped in blue tarp and chains into the cavern. Jurgens is originally from Bois Blanc Island.

Authorities said Jurgens did not resist arrest and led them to the disposal site. "I never hurt nobody," he said while being taken into custody. "The bodies were dead when I got them. I was paid to clean up the mess."

Jurgens oversaw body disposal as part of a statewide underground network that supplied thousands of undocumented workers to farmers, orchard growers, building contractors, road crews, landscapers, and other businesses in desperate need of inexpensive labor.

When the workers died from disease, farm accidents, traffic mishaps, fights, or murders, a specialty business was developed to dispose of bodies from across Michigan, Ohio, and Indiana. Police say that was Jurgens's job. For lucrative fees, he coordinated the efforts of several charter boat captains on Lake Michigan and Lake Huron to dump bodies near Mackinac Island in deep waters beyond the reach of divers and sport and commercial fishing operations.

"No idea how many bodies are down there—hundreds, maybe as many as a thousand," Jurgens said Saturday while awaiting arraignment. "We been dumpin' there for years. I grew up on Bob-Lo. I found the cavern when I was a kid."

Alvarez, a native of Mexico, had been working legally on a visa as a hostess at one of Mackinac Island's swankiest resorts. But officials said she was fired from her job for an employee conduct violation. The firing meant she lost her work visa and was required to return home.

Instead, Alvarez sought employment at one of the large dairy farms in the Thumb. She had amassed a mountain of debt while out of work. To pay it off, immigration officials say, she entered the dark and dangerous world of undocumented workers trying to make a living in this country, where they have no rights and few protections.

"Once you go underground, you are at the mercy of human traffickers and predators who peddle flesh to a wide variety of businesses, some legal and some illegal," said Agent Phillip Stevens, a field officer for the US Department of Immigration and Customs Enforcement (ICE). "It's a harsh and brutal world. Unfortunately for Ms. Alvarez, she knew too much about the body disposal scheme and was considered a problem. We believe that's why she was killed."

On the same day that the Coast Guard pulled bodies out of the underwater graveyard near Mackinac Island, authorities in Grand Traverse County raided an illegal resort called a hotello—part hotel, part bordello, part casino, part drug and alcohol haven—located in what was thought to be a large abandoned warehouse in Traverse City, near the former state mental hospital at one time called the Northern Michigan Asylum.

Alvarez had worked at the hotello briefly before she was killed. She was found with her head bashed in and her throat slashed. A northern Michigan medical examiner discovered Alvarez's identity when he removed her breast implants and traced them to a black market clinic.

Deputy Delbert T. Pickens, a detective with the Emmet County Sheriff's Office, directed the investigation into Alvarez's death. Pickens said two *Blade* reporters were instrumental in putting together the pieces of the puzzle that led to the discovery of the underground network as well as the underwater graveyard.

"We had to backtrack to figure out what happened to Ms.

Alvarez," Pickens said. "The reporters traced her steps from Mackinac Island to the Thumb to Traverse City. They helped Ms. Alvarez's sister, Monica, who came here to claim her sister's body and send her back home. Monica would not give up—she was hell-bent on finding out why Suzie was killed. She's as tough and determined as they come."

Pickens explained that when Monica got too close to discovering the human trafficking network, she was kidnapped and sent to the Traverse City hotello. Monica and another female captive escaped Saturday just after noon.

In another development related to the case, Deputy J.R. Ratchett, a detective with the Huron County Sheriff's Office, arrested Janene Ortiz Saturday night as she was about to flee the farms where she worked in the Thumb of Michigan. Ratchett said Ortiz had several thousand dollars in cash and a plane ticket to Argentina when she was detained near Sandusky in Sanilac County. The ticket indicated she was scheduled to fly out of Toronto.

"I need to give a big shout-out to Agent Stevens of ICE," Ratchett said. "They have been investigating the illegal labor network run by Ortiz and her right-hand man, Juan Perez, for years. But nobody had any idea they were accepting and dumping bodies. That caught us all by surprise."

Perez was taken into custody in the business offices of the hotello. Deputies said he had been clawed and beaten and stabbed in the leg when he was found. They say they have no idea how he received those injuries.

"Looks to me like he lost a fight with a mountain lion and then fell on a screwdriver," Deputy Pickens said. "We made several arrests at the hotello, but there were no patrons at the time of the raid."

Coast Guard officials will continue exploring the underwater cavern in Lake Huron for bodies, which are tied together in groups of four or five and attached to cement blocks. Officials said some of the bodies discovered so far had been in the watery cemetery for years.

Huron, Sanilac, and Bay County sheriffs' deputies helped the immigration department take more than two hundred undocumented dairy farm workers into custody on Saturday. ICE officials said they would be processed and most likely deported. They are continuing to look for others who fled during the roundups.

Chapter 37 — Monday morning

Nick and Tanya walked into the lobby of St. Mary's Hospital in Saginaw and checked with the front desk to find the new room for Sister S., who had come out of her coma Sunday night during a prayer marathon.

The nun, who was about to receive Last Rites from a priest, had rebounded almost as soon as Maria and Monica arrived at the hospital Saturday afternoon. Monica joined the other nuns in reciting the rosary and Maria put her arm around the nun's shoulder and whispered to her. Nurses said they noticed an immediate change in the nun's vitals.

Late Sunday, Sister S. came to, gripping Maria's hand back and moving in her bed. When the nun's eyes opened, she said, "JESUS, MARY, and JOSEPH! Who died? And why are there lit candles and a shrine in this room?" She remembered nothing from the accident that threw her pickup into the ditch and got her airlifted to the hospital.

Those in the room, most of whom had kept vigil for Sister S. for days, rejoiced at her recovery. Sister P. declared it a miracle. Tanya saw it as a blessing. They applauded and whistled, high-fiving each other and praising the Almighty. Tanya called Nick, who was at the office finishing his articles for Monday and Tuesday.

The new room for Sister S. was still in the intensive care unit, but she had been taken off the hospital's unofficial death watch list, which only doctors and high-level nurses had access to. Maria hovered over Sister S., their bond still tight, though it was about to be stretched.

Maria was returning to Mexico with Monica, who had convinced her to go back home and then reenter the United States legally. Both women wanted nothing more to do with the frightful underground life that many undocumented immigrants got pulled into. When the idea was proposed to Agent Stevens after the raid at the hotello, he gave it his blessing, though it veered wildly from federal protocol. He looked the other way— literally—while the women slipped out of the ambulance and hitched a ride to Saginaw.

When Nick and Tanya entered the nun's room, they saw Maria feeding Sister S., who took a break from the midmorning snack to give her visitors a big hug. She had seen Sunday's newspaper, she said. It was the talk of Bay City, Saginaw, Midland, and the Thumb.

"Nick, you are my hero," the nun said, hugging the reporter so hard that they all thought she might fall out of bed. "We had the sense that there were evil happenings in Janene and Juan's world, but we had no idea it extended to the disposal of bodies. Suzie's disappearance broke our hearts. Maria and I loved her."

As they talked, Monica walked into the room to pick up Maria for the journey home and say goodbye. She heard the nun's words about her sister.

"I loved her before you two did," she said, a big smile bursting through. She hugged Sister S. and sat on the edge of the bed across from Maria. The three women reveled in each other and their memories of Suzie.

Nick pulled Tanya out into the hallway. They decided to let the three women spend a little time together because Monica and Maria would be leaving soon. But he also needed to talk with his fiancée— they had important matters to discuss.

"I'm happy this worked out so well for Monica and Maria," he said as the couple found a place to sit in the hall. "When they disappeared without a trace, I was afraid we'd lost them."

"Me too. Sister S. running off the road and the two women

gone—almost at the same time … I had this horrible feeling they were dead or dying. I didn't say anything, but I really started to worry about you and Dave."

"Ah, we were okay." Nick leaned forward in his seat with his forearms resting on his knees. He stared at his shoes. He had brushed off Tanya's concern for her benefit, but he had been very worried, especially when the threat came to the newsroom and his boss was ready to pull him off the story.

"You know, I'm going to have to thank the publisher for not only standing behind us all the way but also spurring us on to complete the story," he said. "Her speech in the newsroom was inspirational. I thought the timing was right on the mark too. It flipped over the skeptics in the newsroom—and the proof is in the Sunday package. Very good stuff, and more to come."

A burly nurse with the voice of a drill sergeant marched into Sister S.'s room—time for the nun to get more drugs and rest. Within a few minutes, Monica and Maria came scurrying out after saying heartfelt and teary goodbyes. They vowed to stay in touch and visit within a year.

The women asked Nick and Tanya to walk with them to the parking lot, where a new rental car was loaded and ready for a cross-country trip. The foursome was silent as they snaked their way through the mammoth hospital.

Maria was the first to speak. She was still wobbly from her ordeal but eager to leave Michigan and go home. She thanked Nick and Tanya for all they had done, getting emotional when she recalled the escape from the hotello.

"Please, thank Courtney for us," she said, choking back tears. She handed Nick a sheet of paper with Monica's contact information. "I want to stay in touch with her. We both do. We will see her when we come back."

Monica fidgeted with her purse for a moment, then glanced at Tanya and asked her if she could hug Nick. Tanya nodded and smiled. "I like hugging him too—when he isn't off working on a story somewhere."

The women laughed. Maria stepped forward and hugged Nick, and then it was Monica's turn. She pulled him in with both arms and spoke quietly into his ear.

"I do not have the words to thank you enough," she said. "I came here to this strange land to find justice for my sister. I couldn't have done it without you. Nate was right. You are a hell of a reporter and an even better man. You were true to your word. Now my Suzie can rest in peace, and her killer can rot in hell."

"You're welcome." Nick smiled. "This was a tough story—and a dangerous one—all the way around. I'm pleased that you and Maria came out of it okay, and I'm happy you're taking her under your wing. She needs that, and it's good for you too."

Now the foursome hugged, forming a square next to the rental. They sobbed and hung on to one another because of the experience they had shared and because they had triumphed over evil—over those who made money from human trafficking.

Monica broke up the lovefest because it was time for the two women to go. Nick and Tanya said goodbye and encouraged them to return for a visit.

As the two turned out of the parking lot, Tanya wiped her eyes and even Nick blew his nose. It had been an emotional morning, enough to tug at the heartstrings of Hannibal Lecter.

The events of the last several days had weighed heavily on Nick. People he had gotten close to had very nearly lost their lives. The physical threat to himself, which he had received periodically over the years, affected him differently this time because of the life he and Tanya were planning together. Over the last few days, he had come to this conclusion: Don't put off the most important things in life. Do them now while you can.

Before they climbed into the Firebird, Nick handed an envelope to Tanya, who looked puzzled.

"I've made you two promises, and now I'm going to keep both," he said, urging her to open the envelope and examine the contents. "We're getting married next week, and we're going to Key West. I love you, Tanya, and I want to make you happy for the rest of your life."

"Ah, Nick!" Tanya leaped into Nick's arms, and they kissed. "You are the best. Will love you forever."

Nick opened the passenger's-side door of the Firebird, and Tanya slipped into the leather bucket seat. As he walked to the driver's side, he said to himself, "Got kissed by the woman of my dreams and hugged by two other gorgeous women. Not a bad start to the week."

THE END

AUTHOR'S NOTE

Thank you so much for sparing some of you precious time to read A Place for Murder. When I started writing about the reporting and life adventures of Nick Steele, I had no idea there would be a book four. Here's something else even wilder. Book Five is already in the works. It's title: *Murder, Key West Style.* Tanya and Nick tie the knot on a beach at sunset, but it's a wedding like you've never experienced.

Once again, I want to thank you for reading my work. If you enjoyed *A Place for Murder*, I would be extremely grateful if you left a review for it on Amazon.com. Good reviews are very helpful in the success for a book. The review can be one sentence, one paragraph, or a page or more. Simply state what aspects of the story you enjoyed. It would truly mean a lot.

Thanks again, my friends.

Until Nick gets pulled into another murder …

Dave

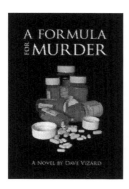

**A Formula
For Murder**

**A Grand
Murder**

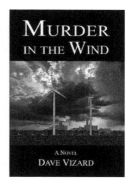

**Murder
In The Wind**

Book club and writer's groups

Dave loves to hear from readers. Don't hesitate to send him a note at davidv1652@gmail.com about anything and everything. He will be glad to answer all of your questions.

Dave also enjoys meeting with readers to hear their observations and discuss their feelings about his books. In addition, he likes working with writers. The Huron Area Writer's Group, an informal organization that Dave co-founded, has been instrumental in publishing his works.

Contact Dave if you would like him to visit your book club or writer's group in person or via Skype. Find out more about Dave at: www.davevizard.com or by visiting his Amazon Author's Page.

Notes for book club

1.

2.

3.

4.

5.

6.

Made in the USA
Columbia, SC
21 June 2023

18054816R00130